Stolen

Stolen

Susan Blackhall

Published by S Blackhall

Back cover image Colin Hill

STOLEN

ISBN 979-8-642-49285-7

Book formatted by www.bookformatting.co.uk.

Contents

About the Author

Susan Blackhall is a retired Mounted Branch police officer from the Metropolitan Police force and, having taken a particular interest in equestrian crime, she is qualified to write, with some accuracy, this fictional tale of crime and intrigue. She introduced a system of marking tack and saddlery to make stolen items easier to identify. It was very similar to that of pedal cycle marking popular in the 1980's. She has police experience in recovering a stolen pony from a council traveller site and searching for stolen saddlery, by attending the weekly horse fair in Southall and the annual horse fair at Stow-on-the-Wold in Gloucestershire.

During her police service, Susan was a regular contributor to 'One One Ten,' the magazine for Metropolitan Police Mounted Branch. She retired to get married to Richard in 1992, moving to the West Midlands with her two horses, a hunter and a Suffolk Punch, and a cat. She immersed herself in the newly formed Midland Heavy Horse Association editing their newsletter 'The Whisperer,' for over 10 years.

Since moving to the Midlands, Susan and Richard have looked after their fourteen-acre smallholding where they currently keep Daisy, a retired gypsy trotter, a working cat called Rosie, a small flock of Soay Sheep and a few Large Black pigs, helped by Otis and Diesel, the Jack Russell terriers. She has spent some years editing 'The Blackmail' which is the newsletter for the Large Black Pig Breeders Club,

Susan describes her career as 'From One Pig to Another,' referring to being a police officer in London before going on to keep pigs on Kinver Edge.

Introduction

A story all about stolen horses. This is not so much a 'who done it' but more of a 'how to catch who done it'.

Set in the West Midlands in 1980, the story begins with two stolen horses being offered for sale at a horse market, and the purchase of a third horse as a birthday present for twelve-year-old Sarah. She and her sister, Lucy, who is a police officer in the West Midlands, become involved in the recovery of the two stolen horses.

Further thefts in this crime wave come closer to home, and Sarah is dismayed to have her own pony stolen. This drags the girls unwittingly into the world of unscrupulous travellers and horse dealers, where they are met with intrigue and violence.

Other children at the stables have some comic interaction with some wild pigs that are running loose. The pigs continue to cause further havoc resulting in meeting Petra, a girl on the run.

Lucy's boyfriend, Steve, helps them with their quest to track all the stolen horses down. He is also a police officer and, together with a friend who travels the markets selling saddlery, they liaise with officers of the mounted branch in London, well known for their expertise in equestrian crime.

Will Sarah get back her much-loved pony, Magpie?

What will happen to the wild pigs, and will they be captured before someone is seriously hurt?

Written for my pony detective

Granddaughters, Jessica and Charlotte

Chapter One

A Pony for Sarah

"Another pony!" the auctioneer shouted, consulting his list before continuing to address the crowd. The back end of a liver chestnut horse, with three dark spots on its rump, disappeared out of the sale ring. "Please note, gentlemen, that lot number fifty-three is not here today, and so we can mark it as 'not forward.' Here we have lot number fifty-four, a coloured mare. What's it worth, you tell me?" He looked around the motley crowd gathered round the sale ring, huddling and muttering as they viewed the next item on sale. Bevan Cooper, or at least that was the name he was using on that particular day, stuffed his hands into his pockets, squeezed himself between tightly pressed bodies, and left the sale ring. He was wholly satisfied with a good day of trading.

It was early in February 1980. He had sold both the ponies that he had brought in to sell, and they had sold for a satisfactory sum, so he was extremely pleased with that, but then they were both stolen, and had cost him no more than the petrol to transport them to the sale. One of the ponies had a freeze mark, making identification easier, as the registration number is clearly visible, picked out in white hair in the middle of the back where the saddle fits.

Bevan was confident that no one would see the freeze mark, because he had covered it over with some boot polish, the same colour as the horse. Anyway, the horse would be long gone by the time it was discovered or, more to the point, he would be. The auctioneers paid out cash on the day and, although they did keep a

1

record of vendors' names and addresses, there was nothing to stop those details being false; which they were in this case and, as nobody knew him in Gloucestershire, he could tell them what he liked, and they would be none the wiser.

He was a stranger to these parts, but he knew that one thing was nationally consistent, and that was the policing of stolen horses was haphazard at best. His contempt for the efforts of the boys in blue left him in no doubt that he had just executed the perfect crime. Becoming aware of the growing hunger in his gut, and ready for a mug of hot tea, and maybe a bacon and egg sandwich, he lumbered toward the sale room café, a lively hub, all spit and sawdust with the occasional terrier tucked onto a grubby knee.

Back in the sale ring the auctioneer was getting into his stride with the never-ending queue of ponies and horses waiting to go under his hammer. "Never raced or rallied." The auctioneer announced, and the smart coloured mare kicked the shavings in front of her as she was led around the tiny arena, alert with fear. Her ears flicked in all directions trying to make sense of the situation. She felt claustrophobic; the faces of strange people crowded in on her with their smelly bodies filling her nostrils. The auctioneer seemed so high above her, like a bird of prey circling before the dive. But it was she who was circling, round and round; she was becoming giddy. The crowd was silent, only the auctioneer spoke in clipped half sentences. "One hundred and ninety I have, one, nine, zero!" He pointed into the crowd at a rough sort of dealer chap waving his bidding card. "Does anyone care to give me two hundred!" "He's against you now, Madam. Make a bid and I shan't dwell." The auctioneer looked directly at two sisters leaning on the front rail. "Thank you, Madam." He acknowledged their bid. "Two hundred, I have. Now folks, let's make it two hundred and ten. Anyone?" He scanned the room for movement, however slight, and the crowd stared back at him, high in his rostrum. "This is cheap. Take her home and surprise the wife. Who wants her?"

"Two hundred and five." The dealer chap bid, and Lucy swung round to see if she could identify the person who had the cheek to bid against her.

2

"I'll accept that bid, thank you." Lucy's face had the look of irritation." Look at her, she is in her prime." The auctioneer continued. "Who wants her, two hundred and ten, anyone?" The sisters looked at each other, their faces engulfed in serious concentration. Lucy nodded and flicked her catalogue at the auctioneer. "Thank you, Madam, two hundred and ten I now have." He moved his eyes round the semi-circle of buyers who were hanging on his words. "Does anyone want to make it more?" With eyes like that of a raptor, he peered into the weather-worn faces. "Are we going any further, gents? And ladies, of course," he added, looking directly at Lucy and her little sister. "All done then, two hundred and ten guineas" and his gavel fell onto the oak base to seal the deal. "What name is it please?" He said as he leaned over the edge of his ivory tower.

Lucy gave her little sister a nudge, "Come on, you tell the nice man who you are." It was, after all, now her pony.

"Sarah," said Sarah.

The auctioneer smiled, "I'm Sarah, fly me?" he teased the nervous twelve-year-old, and the crowd laughed. "Do you have a surname, sweetheart?"

"Oh yes, um, I'm sorry, Sarah Mathews," she said, her face alight with excitement as the auctioneer's clerk scribbled her details onto the clipboard. Sarah bit her knuckles, the white ivories grinning with delight; her big sister put a supportive arm around her shoulders, as the two girls exchanged Cheshire Cat grins at each other.

The next pony entered the ring and the auctioneer informed the crowd that this was a better one than the last.

As the crowd laughed the girls were oblivious to his banter, full of thoughts only for their new pony. "C'mon on, let's go and look at her," said Lucy, and they weaved their way out of the sale ring as the next lot number was treading the same circle as all the others had done.

"What are guineas?" Sarah asked.

"It's a bit old fashioned now, but before decimalisation it was one pound and one shilling," Lucy explained. "To be more accurate these days, it is one pound and five pence. In reality, it just means that the pony has cost us an additional five quid, so nothing to worry about."

* * *

Out on the horse lines where the ponies and horses were penned, in what would normally be cattle pens on many another sale day, their pony stood, solitary and forlorn after the excitement of such a crowded space.

Sarah went into the pen, talking softly, "Hello, little girl, do you want to come home with us?" She turned to her sister. "How are we going to get her home?"

"I am sure we will find someone going in our direction, but we had better not waste any time, the end of the day will come soon enough and some folks are already departing."

"Look at her Lucy, isn't she sweet." Sarah ran her hands over the mare and through the heavy winter coat that she was wearing, feeling down her legs and under her belly.

A voice behind them spoke kindly, "Well done, ladies, you have a good 'oss there." The pony's previous owners, Alf and Trudy, had come bumbling down the aisle.

"Hello again," said Lucy and Sarah. They had spoken at length to them before the bidding had started; the older couple had seemed genuine enough and Lucy had confidence in what they had told her. "We don't have transport for her yet, but I am sure someone will be going our way. Do you come from north of here, by any chance?"

"No, Darling, we're from Devon," said Alf. "There was a guy here earlier that I know, comes from Leek. He's a tall chap, and wears a tartan tam-o-shanter. You can't miss 'im."

"What's a tam-o-shanter?" asked Sarah.

"It's a sort of woollen beret," said Trudy. "It comes from Scotland."

"He's probably still buying, or maybe selling," said Alf, who was in the process of removing Magpie's head collar and stuffing it into a supermarket carrier bag. This act of removing their only means of leading the pony away, was not lost on Lucy. She was a sensible young lady, ten years senior to her sister.

"I thought I saw 'im go for a bit of grub," Trudy said, wishing that she and Alf were doing the same. She nudged her husband, and gesticulated with her eyes towards the two girls.

"What?" said Alf. His wife cocked her head sideways and looked pointedly. "What's up with you?" he asked again, and then the penny dropped. "Oh, yes, yes ok, of course, ok," and he rummaged in his back pocket, pulling out a roll of notes, he peeled away five pounds, and handed it to Sarah. "There you are, Treacle."

"What's this for?" Sarah asked, looking thoroughly bewildered.

"It's called luck money," explained Trudy.

"Have you not heard of luck money?" said Alf, knowing full well that these first timers were unlikely to know the old ways of dealing in livestock.

"You paid a fair price for our 'Magpie,' so we are sending her away with a bit of luck."

"In the world of horses you need a bit of luck," said Trudy.

"If you had bought her cheap, then I would consider that you had had all the luck you were going to get." Alf laughed. "I have sold horses that have fetched very little under the hammer," he continued. "And afterwards, the buyer might come to me and demand luck money. Huh! I told 'em in no uncertain way that they could push off; they'd had all the luck they were going to get."

"It's a good custom." Lucy was impressed. "We like to keep these old customs alive too, don't we Sarah?" And Sarah nodded.

"A good price paid is worth something back in return," Trudy added, nodding with the satisfaction that her husband had done the right thing by these nice young ladies. Taking the five-pound note, they thanked Alf and Trudy for their kindness, and parted company. As soon as they were out of earshot, Lucy told Sarah that she would have to buy a head collar and a lead rope for Magpie. "I saw a big lorry in the car park, which looked like it was selling horsey stuff," she said. "Come on, let's go and investigate that first, in case they are not here all day."

Climbing up the ramp into the back of the Bedford TK, they

5

were overwhelmed by the stock of saddlery and rugs and all things imaginable that might be needed by a horse owner. Sarah saw the carousel of head collars and made a beeline for it immediately. "The prices are good" Lucy noticed, "I would think that she is a cob size."

"Can I help you?" a bonny lady, a little older than them, appeared from the interior of the lorry among the riding boots and hats.

"Polly!" Lucy let out a scream of recognition, the way girls do sometimes.

"Lucy!" simultaneously, Polly did exactly the same thing.

"Oh!" Sarah peered out from behind the carousel. "Hello Polly."

Polly Purse kept the saddlers and feed merchants, 'Horses Galore' on the Clent Hills, and the three girls grinned a welcoming smile to each other.

"What brings you down here? I wouldn't have put you as the horse market sort, Lucy?"

"Sarah had asked for a pony for her birthday, and I was entrusted by Mum and Dad to find something suitable, plus the money to buy it with, obviously."

"How exciting," smiled Polly, "What have you bought?"

"She is a piebald mare," Sarah could not stop smiling either. "She is about fourteen hands high. She is such a pretty pony for a gypsy cob, and not as chunky and heavy as some of them that you see."

"How are you getting her home?" Polly asked.

"We will have to find someone who is going that way. Do you know anyone?"

"Not specifically, but there is bound to be someone going up the M5." Polly was reassuring. "Is this an unsolicited day off school for you then, Sarah?"

"No, I'm not bunking off, honest," Sarah protested.

"The teachers are have a training day today, or something like that, so the school is closed. It has worked well for us though, because we wouldn't have been able to come to this sale otherwise." Lucy explained. "But never mind that, what are you doing here, Polly?" Lucy continued, "apart from selling horse stuff."

"I travel all round, you know, to the markets. I've got a girl working for me who covers the shop when I go to the monthly markets, and the shop is closed every Wednesday anyway, so I can go to Southall, in London, every week."

"It must be worth your while to do this?" Lucy marvelled at Polly's commitment.

"Oh yes, it can be very lucrative. I go to the monthly sales at Kidderminster and Bridgnorth, as well as here at Ross-on-Wye. That's about it, unless something special comes up. Southall is the best though, being weekly you build up more of a clientele, and some of the punters ask me to get stuff for them that is not in stock and I can deliver it the following week. It's a good little earner."

"What about this one, Lucy?" Sarah held up a red collar.

"Hmm, let's have a look." Lucy glanced quickly at the other colours, but nothing grabbed her more than the one Sarah had picked out.

"That would be a good colour on a black and white cob." Polly agreed. So they chose a red rope to match and Sarah parted with the luck money she had just been given by Alf.

Deciding that they had best not delay any further in getting some transport sorted, they said goodbye to Polly and headed off towards the café through the busy thoroughfare. As they went through the double swinging doors to the eating emporium, more canteen than cafe, they spotted their man immediately. He was a rough sort of guy, like so many of those gathered: horse dealers, farmers, travellers, and Irish tinkers. Lucy didn't think much of itinerate van dwellers, 'Do-as-you-Likeys,' she called them, and they were not to be trusted in her view.

"Excuse me," Lucy approached the table. "I am told that you come from the Midlands, Staffordshire way. Would you be able to transport a horse for us, please? She has to go to Kinver."

"Where, in the name of Turpin, is Kinver?" the tam-o-shanter growled at them.

"Um, near Stourbridge," Lucy replied.

He brushed the elastic dew drop from the end of his nose, with the back of his hand and licked the knuckle clean. "Sorry, Gal, I would gladly help you, but my lorry is full."

The girls exchanged a furtive look that spoke telepathically: 'Did you see what he did?' They made their apologies and turned to go, not quite knowing what to do next.

Bevan Cooper was at the next table and had heard it all. This was a good opportunity for him to make an extra shilling on his return journey home. "Hey Ladies! Stourbridge is it? Did you say you wanted to go to Stourbridge?"

"Yes, Kinver." they chorused, stopped in their tracks, they welcomed the unexpected input from this horse thief, who was only marginally smarter looking than the tam-o-shanter. He didn't smell as bad either.

"Take a seat," he invited. "How can I help?"

"We've bought a horse here, and need to get her home," Lucy explained.

"Have you now? That was rash."

"I was sure somebody would be here to help," Lucy continued.

"Can you help us?" Sarah grinned at him winningly. Bevan directed his attention onto Lucy and considered the young lady keenly. Early twenties, he guessed, smart casual clothes, well to do maybe, well educated, and pretty.

"What have you just bought?" he asked hoping beyond hope that it was not one of those he had just sold. They were hot property now, and he had no desire to see either of them ever again. Plus, it wouldn't do to take them back to the area they had just come from. Sarah told him readily, thinking he was interested, but Bevan was more concerned with what the lot number had been. He was relieved when Lucy revealed that it was just a mere two lot numbers after his. A close shave, he thought. "Nice," Bevan muttered absently.

"Do you remember her in the ring, then?" asked Lucy.

"No, I'd left by then." he continued, "I know Kinver. There's nowhere I don't know. Yes, I can take you there, does forty pounds sound fair?"

"That's steep" said Lucy. "Is that the best you can do?"

"If you wanna get home, Petal, you gotta pay. That's the way of the world I'm afraid." And his eyes twinkled back at them above the ruddy cheeks that were filled with sandwich. He ate with his mouth open and tiny spots of chewed white bread hit the Formica surface in front of them, which they politely ignored.

"You are going that way anyway, with an empty lorry at the moment," Lucy persisted.

The words from this cheeky little minx cut no ice with Bevan, a hard-nosed bully boy, he barked back at them, "Forty pounds, or you can stay here for all I care."

"Ok, it's a deal." Lucy should not have been so intimidated, but he was a difficult man to stand up to. "Will you take a cheque?"

"I only deal in cash." He said doggedly. "Take it or leave it." She felt even more uncomfortable, certain in the knowledge that it was not just the pony who would be taken for a ride. "I'll be leaving at two o'clock sharp, I'll see you by my wagon."

"Where is your lorry parked?" asked Lucy. "Or trailer, is it a trailer?"

"No, I've got a lorry, it's the BMC, there's only one parked out there." The girls looked back at him absently. "It has suicide doors," Bevan explained. The girls looked blank. "It's the red one near the gate." Bevan spoke in clipped tones emphasising each syllable.

"Which gate?" asked Lucy, "there are two." Bevan rummaged in his pocket and found the folded catalogue and, tearing a corner off, he scribbled the registration number on the scrap of paper and pushed it across the table towards them. "Oh, that's a good idea," said Lucy, "we'll see you in just under an hour then, um," she hesitated, "thank you"

Bevan got up and left to join the long queue to the auctioneer's window to collect his money, leaving the girls to order mugs of tea and hot breakfast sandwiches.

"We had best see how much cash we have on us, first of all," and Lucy emptied her purse on the table. Sarah did the same, they were five pounds short. "There's one purse we haven't tried, Lucy smiled, "or should I say Polly Purse," she laughed at her own joke, "I bet Polly would lend us a fiver until tomorrow."

"Oh she will, I know she will." Sarah agreed, and they were right, Polly did. It was a day full of blue skies.

Chapter Two

Chestnut Stables

Out in the car park, Bevan waited by the cab of his lorry for the girls to appear with their pony. He was a travelling man, but happily settled these days on a council caravan site near Wolverhampton. Bevan was reasonably happy with his lot, spending his days seeing to what horses he had tethered on common land and the rented odd field in a variety of brown site locations. He was a bit of a wheeler dealer, sharp as a horseshoe nail with his shady deals, a bit here and a bit there, and not all of it legal.

Magpie was easy to lead and meekly followed Sarah and Lucy out into the lorry park. "That's a flashy blagdon you have got there, girls." He greeted them.

"A flashy what, did you call her?" asked Lucy.

"Blagdon, you 'aint heard that 'afore?" he said.

"No," said Lucy, "I would have described her as piebald."

"Yeah, piebald she might be, but a partic'lar type of piebald. She is mostly black with just a few flashes of white here and there, she looks the part with those two white legs. She's nice." He nodded approvingly, as he dropped the ramp down for her. Lucy took the lead rope from Sarah, and led her up into the back of the lorry without fuss or drama. Sarah followed on behind them. There was the stale, sweet smell of old horse muck filling the space and droppings that littered the floor in scrambled lumps. There were no filled hay nets to occupy her either.

Sarah coughed in rejection of the stench, and barely able to hide her disgust she gave Magpie a hug. "We'll be home soon," she whispered into her ear, "and we'll have you out. It won't be for very long, I promise." So with the new pony safely inside, the old blue BMC horsebox pulled out of Ross-on-Wye sale yard followed by Sarah and Lucy in a mustard coloured Datsun Cherry.

* * *

"He's a rough sort, that one," said Sarah as they waved Bevan and his filthy lorry out of the yard at Kinver.

"A nice enough bloke," Lucy replied, "but I wouldn't trust him as far as I could throw him."

"And I bet that's not very far at all," laughed Sarah. They both laughed and turned their attention to the new pony, who was tied outside a stable and patiently watching all that went on around her.

Lucy gave a comforting stroke to the pony's face. "Well, Magpie, you got here safely, didn't you? Not such a trial after all, eh?" It was already dark and the outside electric lamp bathed the yard in soft yellow light, picking out the 'L' shape of wooden stables, and the barn where feed and forage was stored. In the middle of the eight stables, there was a common room with a kettle for making tea, and a microwave for heating up most things. The children who kept their ponies at Chestnut Farm were hooked on Pot Noodles, and the waste bin in the corner of the tea room was usually full to overflowing with discarded cartons. An oil filled electric radiator was a meagre source of heating but still a godsend at this time of year, when frosty mornings and a light dusting of snow were normal.

Sarah couldn't be dragged away from her new pony, and she brushed her all over and, when she had finished, she did it all again, just because she could. Lucy stood by approvingly. This was going to be the making of her little sister, she thought to herself as she disappeared into the tea room to put the kettle on ready for all the arrivals.

Kate, who was Lucy and Sarah's Mother, arrived with the family terriers, Radar and Tetley, who tumbled out of the rear of her car in a whirlwind of excitability, keen to check out the rats in the hay barn, and anything else that wanted supervising. Donna, who was the owner of the yard, drove into the yard with her two children, Michael, a lively eight year old, and Carol, the same age as Sarah. The time had come for the horses to receive their evening meal, and this meant that the yard would very soon be a rabbit warren of activity.

Gill was not far behind them, as her Mother dropped her off at the gate. Gill, Carol and Sarah were the very best of friends and all in the same class at Stourbridge High School. Sarah couldn't wait to show off her new pony, and both Carol and Gill were just as keen to do the admiring.

"Oh!" Lucy suddenly brightened, "I think that is Steve's bike I can hear turning off the main road."

"It does sound like it," replied Sarah and she jumped up and down clapping her hands automatically. Magpie didn't flinch. Sarah liked her sister's boyfriend very much. He was good fun and always made a fuss of her. Steve rode a 1000cc Harley Davidson motorbike, with an engine sound so distinctive that it was famous throughout the world. It was described in words as 'potato, potato, potato'. They listened intently to Steve's bike coming down the lane, 'Potato, potato, potATO, POTATO, POTATO' getting louder before swinging into the yard and crunching on the frosty ground. The terriers kicked off in their usual style.

Radar and Tetley bounced about his feet demanding attention. He bent to give them a brief fuss before shushing them away, and swaggering over to the group who were still fussing over the pony. Steve pulled off his full-face helmet and silk balaclava, shivering at the elements as he did so. He took Lucy's hand and gave her a kiss on the cheek. "Hi, Babe. Well done both of you, this looks like a nice pony. What a lucky girl you are, Fair Sarah," and he ruffled her hair.

"We thought that we would keep her in the stable tonight," Sarah explained. "Tambourine, Cosmo and Debbie all come in, so she can be part of that routine,"

Lucy mused. "She could live out, Sarah, and she probably

always has, she's that sort, but she can stay in tonight."

"We've got to worm her anyway," Sarah pointed out as she untied Magpie and led her into the stable.

"Let's see what tomorrow's weather brings, shall we?"

The electric kettle began to whistle and they retired to the tea room. Lucy set out a couple of motley decorated mugs with a tea bag in each, and added the hot water. A car pulled into the yard and Hayley arrived to attend to Tambourine. Lucy added another mug to the collection

The two terriers leapt out of the easy chairs and threw themselves through the door, barking furiously at the intruder. Recognising Hayley, they hurtled towards her, and the raised hackles were replaced by windmill tails, swirling as if they were about to fly off.

"You have got your pony then," Hayley greeted her friends. "It's a nice looking pony. Does it have a name?"

"Magpie," explained Sarah, "We are not going to change it, they say that would be unlucky."

"Another mare then?" Hayley approved, as all the other horses were mares.

"She is five years old," Sarah told Hayley enthusiastically, "and supposed to be broken for riding and for harness work."

"But time will tell how truthful that information is," Lucy added, cynical as ever.

"She will fit in here very well," Hayley nodded. Her horse, Tambourine, was another coloured cob: a lemon tan and white skewbald. Lucy's horse, Cosmopolitan Heroine, was grey, but would have been whiter than white were she not always plastered in mud.

"At least, if she is in at night," Steve suggested, "you can be more 'hands-on' with her. Just bringing her in and turning her out will be a daily lesson and 'get her in the groove' so to speak." Steve was no stranger to the care of horses, having had his own pony as a child, but he had grown out of them, like so many boys do and, now that he was in his twenties, he much preferred his motorbike,

"I agree with that," said Lucy. "It's just finding the time to manage all of this. I can be here whenever work is not calling," Lucy told them. Like Steve, she was a police officer at Stourbridge police station.

"Who's coming for a drink later then?" Steve asked no one in particular.

"Count me in," Hayley chortled. "We could go to The Cross, we haven't been there for a while."

Lucy noticed that Sarah was pulling a face. "What's up with you?" she asked her.

"Can I come with you, please? I've been in a pub before, with Mum and Dad," she grizzled, as if that was a valid argument.

"Hum," Lucy gave this some thought. "What do you think, guys?"

"Yeah." They agreed it was a special day for Sarah, and The Cross is a family pub. They were blessed with a good number of family-friendly pubs, where even dogs were welcome. The Cross was no exception, with logs burning cheerily in the grate helping the ambience of both hospitality and temperature. So with Magpie settled in a cosy stable, and Cosmo and Tambourine on either side of her for company, plus Debbie, Donna's show jumper, watching the proceedings from the stable at right angles, Steve, Lucy, Hayley and Sarah headed off to The Cross in good spirits.

Steve and Lucy had been a romantic item for nearly a year, but the relationship was not common knowledge to the other policemen at work. If the Chief Superintendent knew about this, then Lucy would be expected to move to a different station, and she did not relish the thought. She liked Stourbridge. She liked Steve. He was fun and he made her laugh and, even though he had no desire to own one, he liked horses too, and that is always a plus.

A harsh tornado of wind blew in through the pub door as Hayley's husband, Dave, came through to join the rest of the gang. Radar and Tetley pulled at the end of their leads to greet him with tails wagging and expectant faces waiting for a fuss. "What's ya' poison?" Steve stood up immediately to buy him a drink. David wriggled into a seat with his back to the window, brown with the residue of tobacco smoke.

"Sarah has got herself a very nice-looking pony." Hayley told him.

"Handsome is as handsome does," said Lucy. "I want to see what she is made of before I pass judgement."

"She's going to be great," said Sarah, "I know, she is. I am so happy, and now I can ride out with you Lucy, and everyone else too. I can ride out with everyone." The thought of riding over The Edge with her sister was an exciting thought. They could now do so much more together.

"How did your test go today, Steve?" Dave asked as his pint arrived on the table.

"Oh my goodness, I forgot about that." Lucy was mortified, her head was so full of ponies and sale rings.

"I passed, thank you. How cool is that? I'm now a fully-fledged panda car driver, and the world is my oyster. Well, Stourbridge anyway."

"Well done, Steve." Everyone congratulated him and he got so many pats on the back he nearly choked on his lager.

"What's the big celebration?" One of the regulars at The Cross enquired.

"Steve is now a panda car driver, so you'd best watch out, Marvin." Hayley teased.

Marvin congratulated him. "We can sleep easy in our beds now, can we?"

"No," Lucy laughed, "it just means he can drive."

* * *

Sarah's school friends had all shared her excitement, when she told them about her new horse. She had some lovely photographs of Magpie to show them. Gill pressed her face against the window of the school bus on Thursday morning, eager to see Sarah and hoping that the film had been developed. The local chemist offered an overnight service and she and Carol waved enthusiastically to Sarah, who was hurrying along to the pick-up point, with her wallet of pictures in her hand and her satchel bouncing about on her back in her haste to get there before the bus.

"Are you lot talking horses again?" Annabelle chipped in from across the aisle.

"Sarah has got a new pony," Gill explained, showing her a picture, "she's lovely, isn't she Carol?"

"She is," Carol agreed, "I think that it is great that we all have ponies now, and we can have so much fun together."

"Our next door neighbour has got two horses," Annabelle said brightly, being keen to be part of the conversation. But her mood changed in a nanosecond, "Or did. She did have two horses until they were stolen the other night."

"STOLEN!" Gill, Sarah and Carol chorused,

"You're joking aren't you?" Sarah asked. Carol shook her head in disbelief.

"No, no I'm not. She was round our house telling my Mum all about it."

Gill looked aghast, "Was she upset?"

"Oh yes, she was distraught," Annabelle confirmed.

"I bet she was," Sarah couldn't believe it. "Where were they kept?"

"Down that road there," and Annabelle pointed through the window to Prestwood Drive as the bus trundled past, headed into Stourbridge. "I go to the tennis club down there; its loads more fun than smelly horses."

"That poor lady. I can't imagine what it must be like to have your horse stolen." Gill was stunned; they all were. "Does she know who took them?"

"No," Annabelle thought that there was no hope of finding them, "Maisie is beside herself with worry, and doesn't think she will ever see them again."

"When did they go missing?" Carol asked.

Annabelle thought for a moment. "She found that they were gone from their field a couple of days ago. Let me think." and she pondered on her thoughts for a moment. "I think that they must have been stolen on Sunday night." They bowed their heads reverently, lost in their own thoughts.

"There used to be a Maisie, with two horses at Chestnut Farm," Sarah added absently. "She was nice, I liked her, but she had a blazing row with Donna and left in a huff. I don't know where she went."

"You're right, Sarah," added Carol. "I remember her, Maisie Evans. "She had two nice horses, Jack and Amber. Didn't she keep them at ours for free, in return for working for my Mum?"

"What did she do?" Gill asked.

"Oh, she used to muck Mum's horse out for her and pick the droppings up in the field. She used to groom our ponies for us and get them ready for us to ride, and get Mum's horse ready."

"No, I mean what did she do to have a blazing row with Donna?

Sarah chuckled, "It was quite funny really. Donna wasn't happy. She had Debutante entered for the indoor jumping over in Droitwich, and was supposed to be leaving at 9.30am, but Maisie was running late, so the horse wasn't ready on time, and that made Donna late for the meet. She was in a foul mood when she got home.

"I think there had been a few issues before that as well," Carol defended her Mother.

"Yeah, but she didn't have to tell Maisie to leave and take her mangy horses off the yard?" Sarah remembered the day well.

"She said that she was quitting!" Carol insisted.

"Only after your Mother told her she was fired," Sarah laughed.

"I wish I had been there," Gill grinned at them both.

"She tacked Jack, the older horse, up there and then, and stormed out of the yard, leading the young horse behind her, if I remember correctly."

"What? Out onto the A449?" Gill was aghast.

"I think so," Sarah nodded.

Annabelle was being thoroughly entertained by all of this chatter and watched as the conversation bounced back and forth between Sarah and Carol.

"My Mum had to muck out Debbie herself the following day." Carol sighed.

"The poxy mucking out," Sarah insisted, "Maisie actually said that, didn't she? She told her that she could do the poxy mucking out herself, for all she cared." They all laughed. "That's when she flounced out, isn't it, Carol?"

"Mmmm, it was. I wouldn't have wanted to see her have her horses stolen though." Carol said reflectively.

"When did all of this happen?" asked Gill. "I've been at Chestnut Farm for over two years."

"Oh, ages ago," Sarah confirmed, "three years at least. Shame, I liked Maisie."

"Yeah, I did," agreed Carol, "so did Mum really. She was sorry when she left."

"It might not be the same woman," Annabelle suggested, "you never know."

"What were the colour of her horses?" Gill asked sensibly.

"I don't know." Annabel's knowledge of horses was nil. "This lady, if it was your Maisie, showed us a photo, they looked brown."

"Oh it can't be her then," Carol pointed out, "both Maisie's horses were chestnut."

"Isn't that the same thing?" said Gill.

"I'll tell my sister when I get home tonight, and she'll soon find out what is going on." Sarah was confident that there was nothing, absolutely nothing, that her police woman sister couldn't do.

* * *

Sarah didn't see Lucy until she had changed her clothes, and her Mother, Kate, had dropped her off at the stables. Lucy was understandably horrified at this news. She remembered Maisie very well, but they had lost touch. Lucy didn't even have a telephone number for her, or know where she lived. "I'll see if I can get to the bottom of this when I go in for early turn tomorrow," she promised the girls. Maisie must have reported the theft to the police, she thought, even though she had heard nothing about it. She knew that Steve would help her in this quest, and it was excellent timing now that he was a panda car driver, and she resolved quietly to commandeer his help. They could investigate this crime together.

19

Chapter Three

Panda Power

After the sergeant had paraded the troops, and informed them of the events overnight at Stourbridge, Lucy nudged Steve and told him that there was a serious matter she wanted to look into. "Follow me to the front office," she asked him, "I want to have a look in the crime book."

"What for?" Steve was intrigued.

"There have been a couple of horses stolen from Prestwood Drive," she told him. "I want to see if there is a report."

"Really?"

"Yes really, I think I know who the victim is. Can I hitch a ride in the panda with you to investigate this?"

"Yeah, nothing else is happening." There had not been many entries since Monday, so the report was not difficult to find. As Lucy had suspected, the owner of the horses was the Maisie that she knew. Steve was not surprised to find that the initial reporting had been carried out by the home beat officer of that area, Silas Morgan.

"We should ask him if he minds us muscling in on his patch first." Lucy stated the obvious.

"He won't mind; he's lazy as sin."

"He is very good at remembering names and faces. He makes a good home beat officer, and he knows everyone on his patch, the goodies and the baddies."

"Is that a fact?"

"Yes, it's a fact. Don't you go giving him a hard time. He

probably just doesn't know as much about horses as you and me, that's all."

* * *

Pulling out of the station yard in Stourbridge, Steve was driving a police panda car for the first time. His girlfriend, Lucy was beside him, which was a rare treat, because their special friendship was a secret. Nobody at the station even suspected that they were an item. And as far as the rest of 'C' relief knew, they didn't even like each other. It was the perfect cover. Lucy was quite excited at the prospect of doing some real police work with the love of her life. It was going to be so much more interesting than plodding down the High Street looking for out-of-date tax discs, or hiding in the butcher's shop with the hope of catching a driver 'failing to accord precedence' at one of the pedestrian crossings.

"What did you say this lady's name was again?" Steve asked.

"Maisie," Lucy confirmed "Maisie Evans." They swung into Prestwood Drive and bumped along a cart track, well overdue for a metalling. "Goodness," said Lucy, "You wouldn't want to be in need of a pee going down here would you?" Steve smiled. They came eventually to a collection of sheds that passed, unconvincingly, for stables, and hoped that there was someone there who could give them further details of the theft. There was no car in sight and it looked deserted, so Steve swung the panda round to leave. "Wait a moment," Lucy urged him. "You never know, I'll take a closer look." And she jumped out and went over to the gate that barred the way. "Hello-oo." She called out, and a head popped round the side of some corrugated tin and squealed in recognition.

"Hello Lucy! Gosh, what a surprise! I am delighted to see you." Maisie emerged in full view. "We've had some trouble here this week, did you know?"

"Yes, that's why I'm here. You had your horses stolen they tell me."

"The police are more efficient than I gave them credit for! I didn't hold out much hope of a proper investigation, when that idiot turned up on Monday. He knew nothing about horses and didn't seem to want to know either."

Steve got out of the panda and joined them by the gate. "Good morning, Madam." He greeted the victim, adopting his 'I'm a policeman and I am investigating this crime' type of mode.

"Oh, this is Steve," said Lucy dismissively. "Don't take any notice. Stephen, this is Maisie, an old friend of mine."

"I'm so pleased you have come to help me," Maisie did look relieved, "but look, let's not stand out here in the cold. I can offer you a cup of tea, if you would like one?"

"Excellent," said Steve. "I don't know a policeman who turns down a cup of tea." They retired to an old caravan that doubled as a store room for grooming kits and office work. "We both have milk and no sugar, thanks," he volunteered, as they squashed themselves onto the thinly upholstered bench seat, thick with horse hair and bits of straw.

"We thought that no one was here," said Lucy. "There's no car parked up, but I am glad we have found you here anyway,"

"I've got a push bike. I only live a stone's throw away." Maisie handed them both a builder's brew, steaming into the cold air.

"Come on then, Maisie, tell us what happened," Lucy urged her friend.

"Not much to tell really, I turned up on Monday morning and both of my horses had disappeared." Putting the horror of the story into words, Maisie broke down. Lucy extracted herself from beside Steve and moved across to sit next to her, offering a comforting arm around her shoulders. Steve looked down at his notebook, embarrassed, but ready to record any useful information. "It's so awful, my worst nightmare."

"Take your time, Maisie, take your time," Lucy comforted her until she had regained her composure.

"I've put up photographs in the saddlers. I don't know what else to do. I didn't think that the police were interested, and I'm just so relieved to find that I was mistaken."

"I'm interested, Maisie." Lucy said soothingly.

"And me," piped up Steve, "we both are, but it's lucky because we heard of this from Lucy's sister, Sarah. A school friend of hers lives next door to you apparently."

Lucy shot him a look of disapproval. She considered it was better for Maisie to believe that the police were pulling out all the stops and that this was an official visit. Oh well, they would just have to convince Maisie that they would stop at nothing to recover her horses for her.

Maisie acknowledged the good fortune. "Gosh, it can be a small world, can't it?"

"You could give us a description of them," Lucy said. "That would be a start."

"Yes, yes, I will," Maisie began. "They are the same two that I had at Chestnut Farm. Jack, you will remember him, he is the thick-set liver chestnut gelding; about fourteen hands two inches, nine years old. Oh, I can't bear it! I've got to get him back. He will be so frightened. We had such a special relationship."

"I remember Jack." Lucy continued to reassure her. "He had the most fitting name, for a stocky little horse. Stonewall Jackson, wasn't it?"

"Yes." Maisie sniffed, "yes, it was. IS! He's still an IS!"

"I remember him well," Lucy smiled at Maisie's defiance and patted the back of her hand in understanding. "I remember you had another chestnut, a yearling, is that the other one?"

"Yes." More sniffing, "Amber, he is four now, and just starting to go well, I had so many plans for him."

"Didn't he have some sort of unusual colouring?"

"Yes, he had black spots, well, dark brown really, one on the side of his neck, and a cluster of them on his rump. I've got some photographs somewhere here." And she rummaged under the sink and pulled out a lever arch box file. "Look, here we are," and she dug out some curly specimens depicting proud moments of her horses.

"I remember he was quite distinctive. Can I borrow these, please?" Lucy flicked through the collection mentally noting anything that might help, then her eyes fell upon a picture of Jack grazing in the paddock. "My God! He's got a freeze mark, Maisie.

Why didn't you say?"

"Well, your lot have already taken those details. I thought that you knew."

"Ok, yes, you're right, I had just forgotten momentarily. But all this does help; it means he is traceable. So, give me his number again, so I definitely have it with me."

"Five twenty-eight P."

"What about Amber?"

"No, he's not freeze marked."

"Have you rung the freeze mark register to report the theft?"

"No, I wasn't sure if I should?"

"Yes. If someone checks his number when he is offered on sale, then it would show up that he was stolen."

"Then someone would be daft to buy him?" This did not make Maisie any happier.

"Probably not, but he would at least be traceable." Argued Lucy.

"And the hottest property in town, no doubt." Steve, could see a flaw in the system.

"Yep," Maisie spat the word out with the realisation of the danger that Jack was now in. "They would take him for slaughter! Wouldn't they?! Wouldn't they??"

"Let's not worry about something that might not happen." Steve could never understand why women invented problems. But he had to admit secretly that this was of deep concern.

"You did say I could take these photos, didn't you?" Lucy asked again.

"Yes, of course."

Steve suggested that it might be worth asking around to see if anyone had seen anything unusual. "Who is there to ask?" Maisie said. "We are in the middle of nowhere, here."

"You're right, of course you are," Lucy began, "but there are houses at the end of the lane. You never know, we'll knock on some doors."

"What about the garage on the corner? Isn't that an all-night garage?" Steve said brightly. "It's worth talking to them."

"I know you must be feeling desolate at the moment," said

Lucy, "but don't worry, we'll do what we can. Look, here is my phone number at home." She tapped her shoulders to indicate her divisional number. "Six, eight, three, if you ring the station, ask for me in person. Or Steve, you can ask for Steve."

"Police constable four, nine, two, Hemmings," Steve said.

"Anything, anything you hear at all that can help us find your horses, just ring. We'll keep each other in the loop and I will do the same for you." Lucy handed her a page out of her pocket book with all the relevant numbers on. Maisie and Lucy pecked each other on the cheek like old friends renewed, before climbing out of the caravan to leave. Steve was just about to get into the driving seat when he had an inspirational thought. "Can you meet us at The Cross tomorrow night? We'll regroup to exchange information."

"Yes, I can be there," Maisie said, filled with renewed hope. "What time?"

"Seven o'clock," said Lucy. "We'll see you there at seven." Steve drove back down the bumpy lane, except that this time Lucy was feeling the call of nature and she was fervently rueing the prediction she made earlier. "I really do need a wee now," she told Steve, "can we go straight back to the station, please?"

"Certainly, M'darlin,' I'll step on the gas." And he bounced the panda energetically down the drive, taking in as many of the different pot holes that he could find on the way.

"Steve! Don't be so mean!" Lucy shouted at him. "That's not what I meant."

Steve laughed, there was much pleasure to be gained by teasing his girlfriend, and he could be so naughty sometimes. "Ok, ok, I'll slow down, but we must come straight back to knock on those doors. There's not much to go on after all."

"There's more than you think." Said Lucy.

"Oh really?"

"Yes," Lucy couldn't wait to tell him. "When Sarah and I were at Ross-on-Wye sale yesterday, we saw a chestnut horse in the sale ring with those dark brown spots. One on the near side of its neck and I saw at least two on the rump. Not small spots, big ones about the size of a ping pong ball. I noticed it at the time because of

Maisie's Amber. I remembered him as a yearling, but I had no reason to think that the horse in the ring might be hers. It just had similar markings."

"Hmmm," Steve was thinking. "The timing is right, anyway. Stolen Sunday, sold on Tuesday. There is a horse market I have heard of in London, on Wednesdays, that's a possibility"

"Yes, Southall." This was a light bulb moment for Lucy. "Polly Purse goes there every week. We saw her at Ross-On-Wye, when Sarah bought a head collar and rope for Magpie."

"That's the one." Steve mused. "It would have made more sense for them to have taken Amber there. They pay vendors cash on the day so anything can be sold and there is no trace of who has sold it." He paused. "Perhaps that's what the thieves would expect us to think."

"How do you know all of this?" Lucy asked.

"I've got a cousin in the Metropolitan force. He is stationed at Southall. We had a family gathering at Christmas, remember? You were there."

"Indeed, I was."

"He was telling me that they have a big problem with the dealers flashing along the High Street with their ponies."

"Doing what, exactly?" Lucy was aghast. She imagined a gypsy dropping his trollies while riding a horse.

"Flashing." Steve continued. "It's running their ponies up the centre of the road through the busy High Street to show prospective buyers how well they can move. They are particularly fond of ponies that pick their knees up high. 'Stepping ponies,' they call them. Anyway, it causes a lot of disruption, as you can imagine, and the police down there have a zero tolerance on the practice. They arrest them if they can for breach of the peace, but that's the best they can do."

"Breach of the peace? That's a bit convoluted, isn't it?"

"There's no specific offence to say that you cannot trot your horse down the High Street." Steve seemed to know all about it. "I'm a bit jealous of my cousin. I would love a posting like that."

"I bet it wakes up the Asian community." Lucy had heard of

Southall. She had heard that it was famous for its delicious curry houses and shops full of Middle Eastern spices and herbs. She imagined that it was similar to some parts of Handsworth, near the West Bromwich Albion football stadium. Steve and Lucy were regular visitors to 'The Baggies,' in uniform obviously.

"It sounds much more exciting than the life we have up here," Steve said.

"Really?" Lucy felt protective about the provincial police force that she served. "We have our moments up here. Your cousin wants to try walking the beat at 1.30a.m. when they are turning out from the All Pink Club on a Friday night." Lucy's thoughts strayed to those evenings. She was disgusted at the thought of drunk youngsters falling into the street. A revelry of party and pop music, loud as you like, and the boys thinking they were men, tumbling and scuffling amongst themselves trying to fight in a frenzy of inability. The words of the much-loved Johnny Cash song were in her head while she spoke. 'Kicking and a' gouging in the mud and the blood and the beer.' She continued, "Huh! What do the Met know, down there, full of demonstrations and ceremonials, paying lip service to the great and the good. We could show them a thing or two up here."

"I doubt it," said Steve. "From what my cousin was saying, they think that all we do up here is chase sheep rustlers. I've never even heard of sheep being rustled round these parts."

They pulled into the back of the police yard and Lucy leapt out, all pith and moment, and ran for the ladies' toilet, two floors up. Steve watched her gallop off and he couldn't help thinking that she was just about the cutest thing he had ever seen.

He was not in his panda waiting for her when she came down, so she went in search of him and found him in the canteen, with a cup of tea in front of him and one he had got for her. "Time for a tea break," he said, like they hadn't just had one, and he invited her to sit with him.

Lucy sat down. "We mustn't let the grass grow under our feet," she said, "Can you ask your cousin who the auctioneers are at Southall and we can give them a ring. We need to do this soon while memories are fresh. I know that I saw a horse that looked like Amber at Ross, but it is not to say that it was him. I could give Cox, Brightworths and Cox at Ross-On-Wye, a ring anyway. Not sure what I'd say, though."

"Hello, you two," Chippy Carpenter, from their relief, sat down next to them. "You two are talking now are you?"

"Only just," said Lucy, shooting Steve a mock look of distaste.

"Tisch. I'm not sure if I approve of these women joining our ranks. Where will it all end? We're stuck with them I suppose" said Steve with false disapproval. With only three years' service, he had no idea of what the job had been like before the integration of women police officers. It was only five years earlier that women police had been a separate department specialising in women and children.

"So, what have you been up to this morning?" asked Chippy.

"Well," began Lucy, "we've been investigating stolen horses as it happens. Have you heard anything about this? It happened during Sunday night, down by the tennis club."

"Nope," said Chippy. "Did you pick it up from the crime book?"

"No, we didn't," said Steve. "There was just some gossip going around. I know Lucy has a horse so I took her along for her professional expertise."

"Did you indeed," Chippy smiled a suggestive smile that said 'there's more to you two than meets the eye.'

"Lucy," Steve had a sudden thought, "If you are right in thinking that Amber had gone through the sale ring at Ross-on-Wye, then it was reasonable to assume that Jack had been there as well. C'mon, let's go to the home beat office and make our phone calls from there."

"Silas might be there as well, so we can kill two birds with one stone." Lucy thought that this was a good idea. She hoped that he had made some enquiries of his own and might have information to add. "You never know, he might surprise us." She added as they trotted along the corridors to the epicentre of Stourbridge policing. "Why do they call him Silas?"

"It's an acronym for 'Sorry I'm late again, Sarge.'"

* * *

They found the home beat office was empty, much to Lucy and Steve's pleasure, and they settled down to try and get hold of Steve's cousin, George. Steve thought he was most likely at work, so he decided to try there first. He rang the number and a London accent answered it. "Is it possible to speak to police constable George Hemmings?" He asked.

"He's is out on patrol at the moment, can I ask who's calling?"

"PC Hemmings," replied Steve.

"Oh, I am sorry, I thought that you were asking for PC Hemmings."

"Yes, I am," Steve chuckled. "I am actually his cousin, but this is not a private call. I'm the 'West Midlands' Hemmings." They both laughed at the stupidity of the situation, and the Southall officer promised to pass on the message.

Steve and Lucy sat and pondered for a moment before discussing their further options, and Lucy thought that a phone call to the auctioneers at Ross-on-Wye would tell them who Amber had been sold to, if only she could remember the lot number. If indeed, it was Amber that she had seen. A four-year-old horse would have looked a lot different from the yearling that she remembered at Chestnut Farm.

Chapter Four

Close Circuit

Maisie Evans made the bumpy journey down the long track on her push bike to return home. It was on this journey that she considered that she did not have to remain idle in her quest to get her horses back. Indeed, she had been like a caged bird since Monday, wanting to do everything possible but not knowing what. Now she knew. Fired up with renewed enthusiasm after Lucy and Steve's visit, she decided to call in at the garage on the corner and ask them herself if they had seen anything during Sunday night.

* * *

She grabbed a chocolate bar from the shelf and went to the till area. "Fuel?" the rather spotty individual asked absently. Maisie looked out of the window at her bike that she had left, somewhat inconsiderately, leaning against one of the fuel pumps.

"Number three," she told him smiling. The spotty fellow checked the display screen for the quantity taken and saw that it didn't show any.

"Is this a joke?" he asked her. Maisie glanced her eyes towards the pump and he saw her bike leaning there. "That's causing an obstruction." he pointed out the obvious. Maisie had thought that a bit of humour might break the ice and a jolly conversation about the happenings of Sunday night would follow easily. She was wrong. "Can you move that thing immediately, madam?"

"I just wanted to ask you about Sunday night." She explained.

"It's causing an obstruction; can you move it?"

Maisie was rattled. "Obstructing who?"

"Any bona-fide vehicle wishing to fill up their tank, that's who."

"There aren't any out there at the moment."

"Move it," he barked.

"Oh, what's the point?" She slammed her money for the chocolate on the counter and turned to storm out. The manager appeared through the 'Staff Only' doorway as she passed, very nearly colliding with her. Maisie was frustrated. Maisie was upset.

"Are you alright, Sweetheart?" Mr Tempest asked her kindly.

Quickly composing herself, Maisie had another go. "I came in to ask you if you had seen any horse boxes or trailers stop for fuel on Sunday night?" She continued, "I've had two horses stolen from down the end of Prestwood Drive. I know it's a long shot, but if I don't ask the questions, you know, I won't get the answers. I'm at my wits' end, clutching at straws really, but I thought it was worth asking? I'm obviously wasting my time with that moron there," and she lay an accusing finger in the direction of the spotty youth.

"I might be able to help you." Mr Tempest said kindly, seeing that she was clearly in a state.

"Someone might have seen something," Maisie became tearful. "Did you see anything? Well, not you, because it was in the middle of the night, but did any of your staff see…….." she paused, not knowing what to say next, "I've got to get them back, I've got to find them, I…."

"Whoa there, young lady, not so fast. Sunday night, you say?" Mr Tempest was taken by surprise at this emotional explosion. "I had to work through the night on Sunday; we had a member of staff go sick on me, and he is still off sick now, the unreliable little no-good. Anyway, yes, I was here all night. Ummm, we have a Closed-Circuit Television camera trained on the forecourt. Thinking about it, there was a horsebox, probably between 2.30a.m. and 3.30a.m. I remember it because it was an old one. I have a fondness for vintage vehicles, though I don't think this was vintage, it was just old." Maisie clasped her hands to her chest. Could this be a lead? She so hoped so. "I'll check the recordings for you. If you give me your telephone number, I'll let you know. Have you reported this to the police?

"Yes. Yes, I have. They came this morning to take further details."

"Well, this information is confidential really but if I see anything on there of any worth, I'll let you know. It is probably best if you come back here with a police officer if you can, and we can go through it together." Maisie cycled home with renewed hope.

* * *

Back at Stourbridge Police Station, Steve and Lucy were considering their plan of action. Ringing the auctioneer was a good plan and Lucy was trying to remember Magpie's lot number. That would tell her the number of the horse that went under the hammer just beforehand. The horse that she thought might be Amber. She remembered the catalogue they had with them, and rang home to speak to her Mother.

Kate was on the phone and so the line was engaged. Lucy put the receiver back into its place, pulling a face. Kate, at the other end of the line, continued her conversation with the insurance company. All this talk in the house about horses being stolen had alerted her to the fact that Magpie should really be insured. "Arh," she agreed with the broker, third party liability was a good idea.

"For the same premium we can include mysterious disappearance," the brokers explained.

"Mysterious disappearance?" Kate questioned. "What's that mean exactly?"

"It's theft really, but if an animal disappears, we can't assume what has happened until we have some proof. Horses do sometimes escape from fields and go walk-about," he replied.

"Bostin'," Kate replied, in the broad Black Country way of expressing her pleasure, and promised to post off the cheque for the premium later that day. She put the phone down.

As soon as Kate had replaced the receiver, Lucy tried ringing her again. Kate's hand never had a chance to release the handset and it rang. Kate was surprised to hear Lucy's voice, as she didn't usually ring home when she was at work. "Hello, Lucy? Am yo' alright?"

"Yes, I just need some information out of the catalogue from Ross-on-Wye. Can you see it anywhere?"

Kate looked around. It wasn't on the table, or the sideboard where things got put, 'for now.' "It aye here, Bab," Kate replied. "Sarah took it t' skewall, yesterday. I think her must still 'ave it."

Lucy, turned to Steve and relayed the information, "Sarah took the catalogue yesterday, to show her mates at skewall. Mum thinks her still has it in her satchel," she interpreted her Mother's accent perfectly. Turning back to the receiver, she continued with her conversation. "Thanks Mum. I'll be home soon. Can you tell her I would like to borrow it?" Kate knew that Sarah would want to go straight up to Chestnut Farm to see her new horse, and suggested that Lucy see her there. Just then Lucy's personal radio was calling her divisional number; she hurriedly said goodbye to Kate, and answered the call.

The officer on reserve asked the question: "Six, eight, three, are you receiving over?"

"Go ahead, Sierra Bravo."

"There is a telephone call for you in the front office. Are you in the station? Over."

"Yes, I'm in the home beat office, can you transfer it?"

"Doing it now, six, eight, three." And within seconds the phone rang. Steve grabbled the receiver before Lucy could get hold of it and, grinning from ear to ear, he spoke; "Hello?"

"Hello?" said Maisie.

"Hello," said Steve, surprised to hear her voice. "What's new?" Lucy could just make out the muffled sounds of Maisie's voice on the other end of the phone. "That's very good." continued Steve, cupping his hand around the receiver to make it more difficult for Lucy to hear anything. "Ok, well done, Old Thing." He smirked at Lucy in a Secret Squirrel sort of a way. "I see," he continued, "well, that's really interesting." Lucy heard Masie speaking again, and just wished so much that she could hear the details. "Ok, we'll be there,

33

just let us know, and keep us informed." Steve put the receiver back.

"Was that Maisie?" Lucy was desperate to know what had been said. The news sounded promising.

"Wouldn't you like to know?" Steve teased her.

"Stephen! Tell me, you rotter." And she slapped him across the shoulder just as the door open and in walked Silas Morgan.

"OOOoooooOOOOooooo?" he said knowingly, "what are you two doing skulking in here - together?"

"We are following up on official enquiries," Lucy explained.

"Enquiries that you should be making." Steve said pointedly. He could be such a troublemaker.

"What enquiries would those be then?" Silas was now on the back foot, but Lucy quickly explained all that she knew.

She told him of their visit down Prestwood Drive. "Maisie is distraught. We have to help her," she insisted

"It's a no hoper," said Silas. "How can you find two horses? It's like looking for a needle in a haystack."

"Not now it isn't," Steve told him and he shared the information that he had received from Maisie's phone call. "If you are happy to leave this to us, we can keep you up-to date. Obviously, it's your report after all."

"Do what you like," Silas said. "All policing is good, but I've got better things to do with my time than to go chasing about the country after stupid horses." He left the office thoroughly satisfied that he had been spared a wild goose chase.

"You are right," said Lucy, "he is an idiot."

* * *

The end of this tour of duty arrived, and Steve suggested that they call in at the garage on their way home and confirm to the manager that this was indeed a police matter. Out in the yard, Steve fired up his bike and Lucy jumped into her little car, and they went in convoy directly to the garage, where they spoke at length to Mr Tempest. By the time they got to Chestnut Farm, Sarah, hotfoot from school, had collected the terriers from home and was giving Magpie a really good groom. The horse was beautifully marked with a flash of white in the middle of her neck, making that part of her long mane look like lightening against the shiny covering of black. She was mostly black, black as the night sky, with an iridescent glow that dazzled when polished up. Sarah could see all manner of colours in her when the sun shone, purples and blues, reds even. She sparkled with all the bling of a brightly coloured neon sign. Magpie had two long white stockings, a belt of white around her neck and another on her saddle area, and the top half of her tail was white, too. She was a seriously striking little horse. Sarah was making a good job of getting her spruced up and clean; even the smattering of feathers on the back of her legs were free of all the mud that she had collected.

Hayley came out of the tea room when she heard the bike pull in. "I've put the kettle on," she announced, and Steve gave her the thumbs up. "I'll tell you what," Hayley began, "this little horse can't half move. You should see her go! All three of our horses flew round the field like mad things when they were turned out this morning. I don't know how you are ever going to rise to her trot, Sarah. She moves like a Hackney."

"I don't care," said Sarah, and gave Magpie a munchy hug, and Magpie seemed to enjoy that. Sarah put Magpie back into the stable and they all retired to the tea room where Hayley and Sarah were keen to hear about the stolen horses. "Mum said you wanted this." Sarah pulled the catalogue out of her satchel.

"Ah, brilliant." Lucy took it and began to thumb through the pages. She found the page where Magpie was listed and, on seeing it in print, she remembered that the lot number had been fifty-four. She was pretty sure the horse that she thought looked like Amber, was immediately in before her. "Number fifty-three it is then." Lucy put the catalogue down on the table in front of her. "I'll make a quick phone call to the Ross-on-Wye auctioneers, right now," she continued as she picked up the stable phone and dialled the number that was on the front of the catalogue, hoping that their offices were still open.

"I am sorry, we don't give out personal details over the phone." The office secretary told her curtly.

"I am a police officer for West Midlands, WPC six-eight-three, Mathews. You can check out my details."

"I'm sorry, but you could be anyone. How do I know you are who you say you are?"

"This information is necessary for our investigations." Lucy was beginning to get frustrated. "If I discover that you have peddled stolen horses through your sale ring, then I can prosecute your company for perpetrating the crime before the fact." Steve waved his arms about frantically at Lucy, gesturing for her to watch what she said, as this conversation was obviously going nowhere. Anyway, Lucy was talking rubbish; it would be after the fact, not before.

"Well then, you will just have to come into the office in person." the secretary told her, getting more impatient. Lucy assured her that she would do just that, and put the phone down.

"We can go there on Monday," Steve told her brightly. "We are both on weekly leave, and it would be a fun run out on the bike. We can be there in no time." Sarah listened intently, wondering if she was included in these plans. Lucy agreed, although she did think that waiting until after the week-end was two days too long.

"You know, Steve." Lucy began, "we should really go down to Ross tomorrow. We could ask the skipper for three hours' time off. If we finished at 11a.m. we could be down there by noon. I really think that speed is of the essence here."

"Ok," said Steve. "We could do, assuming that the skipper will let us both go."

"We can tell him that these are police enquiries." Said Lucy.

"Ha! That's novel! Performing police duties in my own time!" he laughed. "Who'd have thought it?"

* * *

Sarah had Saturday planned out already. She was looking forward to going with her mum to Horses Galore, and getting Magpie kitted out with a saddle and bridle, rugs and some extra brushes for her grooming kit. There were lots of things she wanted to buy. Lucy should have been going too, being the only one in the family who knew about horses. "What about Magpie?" Sarah injected. "You are supposed to be coming with us to Horses Galore."

"Oh Sarah! I forgot about that." Lucy tutted, "They are open on Sunday morning. Can we go then?"

Sarah just couldn't wait to get on her new pony and go riding over Kinver Edge with her friends. "No!" she shouted. "You promised we would go tomorrow. You promised!"

Hayley saw an opportunity to help, having thus far been on the periphery of the proceedings, and she did want to help where she could. "Sarah! Listen! How's this for a plan? Would you like me to come with you? I can advise you on what is best to buy and, if your Mum can still come too, we can get everything you need for Magpie. If I know Polly though, she will come here and measure Magpie properly so that she has a saddle that fits correctly. It will be fun. I'm loads more exciting than a boring big sister."

"That's a brilliant idea, Hayley." Lucy said brightly. Sarah was unconvinced. Lucy was keen to show Sarah how important this was. "I can then go on the hunt for Maisie's horses. That is important, Sarah. It is important that we act quickly, or we might not get them back."

"Ok," Sarah said rather dolefully.

"We get on ok, don't we?" insisted Hayley. "We have always been good friends, haven't we, Sarah?" She wanted Sarah to be happy about this arrangement.

"Yes, I'm sorry, Hayley," Sarah said politely. "Yes, it will be lovely to go with you, Hayley; you know more about horses than my smelly sister anyway." And she poked her tongue out at Lucy, who cupped her hand over her mouth, grinning widely behind it.

Steve raised his eyes to Heaven. 'Sisters!' he said to himself, quietly.

Sarah whipped out a sketch book and pen from her satchel and began doodling, on a clean page, an image which she thought would look like Magpie. It didn't, but practice makes perfect, she thought, and doodled another, which was a bit better than the last, even though it still looked as though it had been done by a twelve-year-old; which, of course, it had.

The door opened and Maisie came in along with a flurry of frosty air and the terriers, who had been busy ratting in the hay barn. "Hello, you," Lucy was surprised to see her old friend. "You've never cycled all this way?"

"It's not that far, Stourton to Windsor Holloway, took me just twenty minutes. It's cold though, but if I pedal faster I stay warmer," Maisie explained. "My goodness Sarah, how you have grown in the last three years. You were a mere sprog of nine then, I think."

Sarah grinned a welcoming grin. "Hello Maisie," she said. "I am sorry to hear about your horses." Maisie nodded acceptance of the facts and diverted the conversation by asking Sarah about her new horse. They all went out briefly to huddle round the stable door and admire Magpie, before diving back into the comfort of the tea room. Steve got to the armchair before Radar claimed it, and Lucy plonked herself on his knee. In turn, Radar jumped on Lucy's knee and she gave the cutest of terriers a rub around his shoulders and head. Hayley made Maisie a cup of coffee while commiserations were exchanged over Maisie's sad loss, and reassurances that they would stop at nothing to recover Amber and Jack.

"Mr Tempest, 'he of the all-night garage,' has rung me to say that he has some camera footage that we might find interesting," Maisie told them. "How are you two fixed for time? I can't wait to see what he has found."

"We're ok," Steve replied. "I'm keen to get on the case too, you know."

"I can give you a lift, Maisie," Lucy suggested, "Save you cycling, and you can leave the bike here, and collect it later." It seemed like a good plan and, in fact, the four of them went in Lucy's little Cherry, including Sarah who didn't want to be left out of the action, plus dogs, grubby footed and panting with excitement, and smearing the windows with dog snot until they pulled up on the garage forecourt.

"Good, you have all come together, that's brilliant." welcomed Mr Tempest as Maisie, Lucy and Steve and Sarah entered the shop. "Walk this way," he instructed.

"If I could walk that way," whispered Steve to the girls, "I wouldn't need talcum powder." Lucy giggled.

"Here we are," Mr Tempest invited them to sit while he fiddled with the tiny screen that revealed all that had occurred on his forecourt. The film began to roll and in grainy black and white they could clearly see an old BMC lorry pull up alongside pump number five.

"That's Mr Cooper." Lucy leapt to her feet, and leaning towards the screen she scrutinized the image. Bevan got out of the cab and began to fill up with fuel. "Yes, that's him!" She turned to the others, "It's him, it's him!" She was seriously excited now.

"It's who?" asked Steve.

"It's Mr Cooper! He transported Magpie for us from Ross."

"When was that again?" asked Maisie.

"Tuesday." Lucy trembled with excitement. She could not believe that they had hired a horse thief to transport Sarah's horse for them. The tape had now gone past the point of interest and Lucy turned back to the screen just in time to see him drive out. "Can we run that again please Mr Tempest?"

"Certainly," and he rewound the tape to show the images a second time.

"Can anyone read that number plate?" Lucy asked.

"I can see the letters," offered Steve. "It looks like 'Tango, Papa, Hotel." He said, using the phonetic alphabet so familiar to police officers. "Then, three numbers, they might be five, three, and seven.

"It looks like five, five, seven," said Maisie screwing up her eyes.

"Steve leaned forward and offered "I think it's an eight, yes two eights. I think it is eight, eight, seven, and the suffix F for Foxtrot."

Sarah suddenly remembered. "Didn't he give you his registration number at the market, Lucy?" She was wide eyed with this realisation. Lucy stuck her hand into her back pocket and pulled out the scrap of paper that was still there. The same piece of paper that he had written his registration number on, so that Lucy and Sarah could find his lorry.

Lucy read it out, "Tango Papa Hotel, eight, eight, seven, Foxtrot. Bingo!" She exclaimed. "Sarah, you are so clever!" And she leapt up high, not that there was much room for leaping, and she punched the air in exaltation.

"GOT YA!"

They all jumped out of their chairs and congratulated each other on a good job done. Even Mr Tempest, who didn't know the horses, or them before today, seemed delighted to have been some help.

"Can we keep the tape?" Steve asked. "We might need it for evidence if we can ever get this guy to court?"

"Certainly."

"What do you mean, IF?" Lucy asked him.

"This is all circumstantial at the moment, Lucy." Steve was a realist. "We know it's him, that's enough for you and me, but not enough to get him to court; not yet anyway."

"And it's only half the job," pointed out Maisie. "I haven't found my horses yet, and I care more about that than some measly conviction. He'll only get a fine and a few hours' community service anyway."

Sarah could not think of anything worse than having a horse stolen, but she had no doubt that her sister would find them. "We'll find them. We'll find them now," said Lucy. "We have to go to Ross-on-Wye tomorrow, Steve. We have to!"

"Indeed we do," Steve agreed. "Come on, we cannot take up any more of Mr Tempest's time. We cannot thank you enough, Mr Tempest, you have been most helpful. Would you be willing to make a statement and give evidence in court?"

"Certainly," he replied.

Chapter Five

A Shaggy Sheep Story

Late on Tuesday afternoon, the same Tuesday that had seen the sale at Ross-On-Wye, a magnificent mackerel sky had smiled down on the young lady who had bought Jack. Skipping up the path to the house, Stella was delighted with what she had bought. She had settled her new horse into the stable at the bottom of the garden with the other two resident horses, sure that this dear old stalwart would make the perfect quiet hack for her Mother. She was a good judge of horses, but if he didn't shape up as she thought that he would, then he could go back to Ross the following month.

"I bet you are ready for a cup of tea," her Mother said as she walked into the kitchen.

"Indeed I am, Mother." Stella grinned as she sat herself down at the large wooden table and reached across for the welcoming mug. She took a sip and set it back down on the table. As her hands let go of the mug, her eyes immediately fell on the brown smudges left behind by her fingers. It is a funny thing but, until this moment, Stella had not noticed the Kiwi Parade Gloss dark tan stains on the inside of her palms. She looked at her hands in bewilderment. It wasn't mud, or road film from the journey. Where had it come from?

"Is everything alright, Stella?" her Mother asked, noticing the change in her expression.

"I can't work it out, Mum, where all this brown stuff has come from," she said, showing her Mother the stains on both of her hands, and now on the mug.

41

"That will be grease off the tow hitch of your trailer probably," Mother said helpfully, passing her some kitchen roll to wipe it off.

"No," said Stella, shaking her head, "It's the wrong colour." Her thought processes chugged inside her head, "It's the same colour as the new horse, that lovely liver chestnut colour." Her thought patterns spun into overdrive. She had run her hands all over him at the sale, while he stood quietly allowing every invasion of his privacy. The brown stains had come from him, she knew it, and it must have been there to hide something. He has been altered somehow, Stella thought. Something was not right. 'Could he be a ringer?' she asked herself. Leaping to her feet and making a brief apology she went purposely back down to the stables. Her Mother followed on, bewildered, and had yet to catch up with Stella's deduction of the plot. By the time she had got to the stables, the freeze mark had been discovered. "This means only one thing, Mum," Stella said as her Mother's face appeared over the stable door. "This horse has been stolen."

* * *

Far away, near the Forest of Dean, Amber was not best pleased with how the day had turned out for him. He had been squashed into a lorry with a bunch of horses that he didn't know. He had been so roughly handled that he was now frightened of what the future might hold, and the other horses were frightened too. This shared anxiety did nothing to calm them down. He pressed one eye against the gap in the boarding of the lorry. This was a cattle lorry, and he and the other horses were loose, bumping against each other and feeling very unstable. The towns and countryside flew past in front of his eye and he could not make any sense of it. Where was Maisie when he needed her most? Where was his nice hay net which he usually had to occupy him on journeys? Where was Jack, his best friend? Amber's brain was in a whirlwind of disorientation, and the arrival at their destination did not improve his situation. With a flurry of bad temper and kicking, he and the other horses were loosed out into a large muddy paddock. He did his best to stay clear of the flying feet and had to retaliate to protect his personal space. The paddock was cold and icy. He was used to being turned out in a rug but there was no rug on him now, and he was feeling the cold bite into him. Some of the horses huddled together in groups, but he could not find any individuals who would allow him near them. He was in for a very unhappy night. With his tail clamped tight into the crease of his bottom, he turned it into the wind and, with his head down, he braced himself against the weather. He was dejected in the extreme.

"We'll get the measure of these brutes in the next few days, Gavin, and see if we can make a quick turnaround." The two brothers slammed the gate shut to the paddock and walked back to the house, clutching their coats tight around themselves against the unforgiving weather. Horse dealing was a precarious business and decisions had to be made fast. There was no room for niceties, and any that looked like they would not make the grade were sold back through the sale ring pretty darned quick.

"They'll teck n'harm there fer the night." John nodded, satisfied with the day's purchases. Amber watched them go. He was an intelligent horse, and the thought of remaining there in this soulless place was more than his patience could bear. He bravely turned his head into the wind and began to inspect the compound where he was held captive. All the fences were made of wooden pallets up on end and tied together with baler twine. There was the occasional post driven into the ground to add stability but, generally speaking, this was a rickety construction. Amber gave it a bit of a push in places where he thought it was at its worst. Or, in his opinion, at its best. He pressed his back end against it in one or two other places and he felt it give under the strain. It would not take much, he concluded, but the cold was biting hard into his wellbeing, and he wondered if he had it in himself to escape. But escape he must. He didn't trust these rough men, he didn't trust them one little bit and, with a sudden surge of determination, Amber kicked out at the fence. With a crack of splintering wood, the pallet disintegrated, exploding fragments into the blackness. Amber's sharp senses told him all he needed to know and, with a leap of faith into the darkness, he was free and, not surprisingly, so were all the other horses

* **

Back in the police station at Stourbridge on Thursday morning, Steve and Lucy had reported for duty, and their first priority was to get the permission from their sergeant for the time off. Once the reasons were explained, they were allowed four hours, which was great. They could finish at ten o'clock and be at Ross-on-Wye in an hour and a half.

Steve rang his cousin, George, at Southall police station in West London. He wanted to pick his brains about horse markets. There was every possibility that Maisie's horses could get peddled around before finally finding a resting place. Steve was interested to learn from his cousin that there was a squad of policemen from the mounted branch in London, on duty at Southall market every week. George's involvement with the horse sale was limited, but he told Steve that the mounted officers who came were apparently very knowledgeable. They were good thief takers, and had many arrests to their credit and, more importantly, many stolen horses had been returned to their owners. "What they don't know, in the world of horse dealing, isn't worth knowing," George told Steve.

Lucy rang the Police National Computer to do a vehicle ownership check on the registration number of Bevan's lorry and learned that it was registered to a Besnik Claydon, living at a traveller site in Jenny Walker's Lane, just outside Albrighton. Lucy was confused. The location was about right, given that he had transported Magpie on his way to his own home address. But the name? The name was not right at all."

"The name he told you must be false," Steve deducted. "It has to be. I bet ya, the name Besnik Claydon does not appear in any of the records at Ross." Steve couldn't wait to get down there and have some of his questions answered. "All we know so far," he went on to re-cap the evidence to Lucy, "is that the man you saw at Ross-on-Wye, is the same man on the CCTV at the garage, filling up with fuel on the same night two horses were stolen, and in the same location." Lucy nodded agreement. "That's all we have. Sadly, casual circumstances do not stand up in court. C'mon, the time has come, let's get down to Ross-On-Wye." In no time at all, Steve's Harley Davidson was spudding its way down the M5; the 1000cc engine singing a jolly shanty about potatoes. Steve was singing happily too, "A burn up, wiv a bird up, on my bike." He sang as the miles were eaten up and left behind them.

In no time at all, Stephen was flashing his warrant card to the girl behind the glass of the auctioneers' office. The whole of the market was in a flurry of selling sheep and cattle. Fat lambs were being auctioned from their pens. Now nearly a year old, they all looked like they would make a good meal for a discerning butcher to display in his shop window. The market was noisy, the never-ending blarting from the sheep filled the air with a crescendo of volume.

"What can I do for you?" the auctioneers' assistant shouted to Steve through the glass at the pay desk.

"Can I have access to your records for the sale of horses last Tuesday?" he shouted back, but she couldn't hear him correctly.

"What did you say?"

"For goodness sake." Steve mumbled. "Lucy! Can you go and shut that door please?" Lucy did as he asked and immediately silence was restored. The girl behind the glass offered to fetch one of the partners, Mr Cox. "Is that the first Mr Cox in the title or the second?" Steve asked with a cheeky grin. The girl gave him a pained look as though that question had been asked more times than she could count, before she disappeared to find a Mr Cox. He was a portly figure, and listened with great interest to Steve and Lucy's story, agreeing that there could be a possibility that stolen goods were fenced through the sale ring on Tuesday. He was adamant that his company did everything in their power to safeguard themselves against such occurrences. and was reluctant to accept that any responsibility could possibly fall at their door.

"Why do you have to pay out to vendors on the day?" Lucy asked him, as he thumbed through the sale sheets to check the records. But he didn't give a satisfactory answer as far as Lucy was concerned.

"Lot number fifty-three, you think?" he asked, as he turned the right pages. "Ah hah, there was no lot number fifty-three. The horse was not forward, so there's your first error." Mr Cox seemed very pleased with himself. "You've had a wild goose chase, I'm afraid."

"Not so fast," interjected Lucy. "You have jogged my memory. You are right, fifty-three did not turn up. I remember that now. Who was the vendor for lot number fifty-two?"

"Ummm, a Bevan Cooper. We don't know him. As far as I know, he is a new visitor to this market. He sold lot numbers fifty-one and fifty-two. They both fetched one hundred and ninety five guineas. Good money."

"Do you have an address for him?" asked Steve.

"Yes. 31a, Merryweather Road, Luton, Bedfordshire."

"He was a very long way from home then." Lucy didn't believe, for one second, that this address was correct.

"Well, that's the address he gave us," Mr Cox stated, with a pompous air.

"This wouldn't happen if you didn't pay out on the day." Lucy stabbed her finger in the air in his direction. "I rest my case." Mr Cox didn't acknowledge the comment. "Who bought both those horses?" Lucy could barely wait for the information.

"Ummm, that's another sheet," and he rummaged on the desk. "Here we are then. They were bought by different people. Lot number fifty-two was a liver chestnut gelding and he went to Miss Stella Wentworth of 'The Oaks', Coulter Close, Brecon."

"Mmm." Steve and Lucy both scribbled the information in their pocket books.

"Lot number fifty-one. Ah yes, another chestnut gelding. That one was bought by the Bray brothers. They are horse dealers and they are well known to us. They come here a lot. Most months in fact."

"Their address?" asked Steve.

"Yes, of course, Woodhouse Farm, Cinderford, Gloucestershire." Mr Cox was anxious not to offend any of his regular customers. "They won't know the horse was stolen though."

"Of course, they won't," said Lucy. "But we have to recover this property, if we can."

"Not forgetting we have to catch the thief as well." Steve was now hungry to feel Bevan's collar, or should we say Besnik's?

* * *

Out in the sale yard, unbeknown to them, a young man, Lewis Lewis, was bidding for a pen of Jacob sheep. The auctioneer stood high above him on the wooden walkway that divided the sheep pens running in a long line, back to back. Lewis was a beginner, not yet eighteen, and young for his age. He had secured for himself a very good market in the meat from rare breeds of sheep and, on the promise of a small flock of Manx Loaghtans at a knock down price, he had sold them before actually purchasing them. The seller had then become greedy, and the sale had fallen through. Lewis needed some more sheep, any rare breed would do, and he needed them in a hurry. He needed them now. The bidding had been keen and he was reaching the economical limit, but now he was up against just one other determined buyer. Lewis and his rival bid hotly for a pen of Jacobs, and they eyeballed each other between bids. At ten pounds per head of sheep, the pen was in danger of becoming too expensive for Lewis. He bid eleven pounds and said challengingly to his opponent "I'm going to have them."

The crowd fell silent and waited for the other fellow to reply, and the auctioneer looked expectant. "Twenty five pounds apiece I bid." The opposition announced, gesticulating with his index finger towards Lewis, the young upstart. He was sure in the knowledge that Lewis would bid against him and would have to buy the sheep at a far greater value than they were ever going to be worth. It would teach the youngster a lesson he thought to himself, the whippersnapper, coming here, trying to play with the big boys. Lewis didn't bid again, he just smiled and walked away. The crowd laughed like a row of buckets with the delight of seeing one of their number cut down to size by the little brat.

Lewis retired to the canteen where his opponent came over to him and complained. "I thought you said you were going to have those sheep." he barked.

"Not at that price," Lewis replied and carried on eating his double egg, beans and black pudding. The bidder shuffled off muttering obscenities under his breath. Lewis put his cutlery down neatly onto his empty plate, when he was again approached by another man; this time by a grandfather figure, looking kindly at him from behind his bearded face.

"That was a bit of fun," said Grandad, sitting himself down. "You got the better of him, didn't you, Son?"

"Folks think I'm a push-over, if they don't know me better." Lewis replied candidly.

"What you don't realise, young man," Grandad began, "is that the bloke who was bidding against you is a butcher."

Lewis, all fresh faced, beamed a winning smile at him and replied, "What he doesn't realise, Pop, is, so am I." They both smiled kindly at each other in mutual understanding.

* * *

On the way back to his Father's Land Rover and the dinky little trailer hitched to the back of it, Lewis stopped to admire Steve's Harley. He had always been a big fan of Harley Davidson motorbikes and that distinctive engine sound of the pistons, firing level with the passing of every other lamp post in the street. It made the hair on the back of his neck bristle with excitement.

Simultaneously, Steve and Lucy were thanking Mr Cox for all his help and beginning to make their way across the sale yard. As they battled through the gathered throng of eager hopefuls, all of them after that magic deal coveted by farmers and butchers alike, Steve spotted the young lad hankering furtively round his bike. He had only one thought on his mind. After all, he was a policeman, and they can think of nothing else other than the crimes and misdoings of others.

"Oi! What do you think you are up to?" he shouted.

Lewis was quite taken aback. "I'm just looking, mate. Don't get your knickers in a twist."

"I'm not your mate....Mate!" replied Steve and grabbed Lewis by the shoulder to stop him running away, but Lewis had no intention of running away. Why would he? He was not doing anything wrong.

"Let him go, Steve," insisted Lucy, "look, he's only a lad."

Steve let go of him, reluctantly, saying "only a lad, he might be..." Lewis shook himself free from Steve's grasp.

"I bet he's not even shaving yet," said Lucy.

"Yes I am," protested Lewis. "Not very often, granted, but I am shaving." Lucy laughed, Steve was not so sure. He just didn't trust anyone here. "I'm just admiring your bike," Lewis explained. "This is the sort of bike I want to get, when I can afford it."

"Is that so?" Steve asked.

"Yes, of course, it's the engine noise I love the best. You can't mistake them, can you?" Lewis showed such enthusiasm for the machine, Steve began to have a change of heart. With the twist of his wrist, Steve fired her up. "Beautiful!" Lewis was delighted.

Lucy smiled at them, happy that Steve was establishing a better frame of mind with this bright young man. There was nothing wrong with a goodly bit of public relations. "This is a serious bike and no mistake," she said.

"Some aren't," Lewis piped up. "Those Japanese bikes can't be serious for a moment, especially that Yamahahahahahahaha."

Steve tried not to smile, but he couldn't help himself. "You're alright, you are," he said. Spotting the chuck wagon outside the entrance to the sale ring, serving burgers and chips and stuff, he pulled at Lucy's elbow, "Hey Lucy, shall we grab a coffee before we head back?" From where they were standing they could smell the mouth-watering burgers cooking.

"We could do with some lunch too," she said. "Hey kid, do you want to join us?"

"Ok," said Lewis, "I've just eaten, but I'll join you for a coffee." And the three of them headed over to the burger van. Lewis told them about his experience with the sheep and how he missed out on a deal. He told them about his small flock of Castlemilk Moorits and his parent's farm in Aylburton, on the edge of the Forest of Dean. Steve and Lucy told him that they were police officers from the West Midlands, and that they were looking for two stolen horses. They urged him to keep his ear to the ground if he heard of anything, although it did seem that both horses had gone to legitimate owners and alarm bells would not ring. Steve suggested that they drop down to Cinderford before they went home and pay a visit to the Bray brothers, Lucy agreed. "Do you know them, Lewis, they can't be far from you?"

"I've never heard of them," he replied, "Cinderford is miles away from our farm." They parted friends, and, armed with Steve's telephone number, just in case, Lewis set off for home in his Dad's Land Rover, pulling an empty trailer.

Chapter Six
Deal or No Deal

Back at Chestnut Farm, Sarah was polishing Magpie. Again. She just loved to give her a groom and it seemed that they had been friends for so much longer than just two days. She had been to Horses Galore with her mum and Hayley, and bought a lovely English leather snaffle bridle, along with a winter rug and lots of other things. Polly Purse arrived in the afternoon, and her car was stuffed with saddles, new and second hand. This was yet another day of discovery for Sarah and she just couldn't wait to get going. She was a good little rider but her experience was limited. Lucy had volunteered to be the first to get on Magpie, but right now Lucy was on a mission in Hereford with Steve.

Polly fitted Magpie up with the saddle that she thought would be most suitable, and they led her out to the grass arena that was fenced off to make a passable outdoor manège. The terriers tumbled into the area ahead of them and busied themselves trying to get underneath the pile of jumping poles stacked at one end. Sarah held the reins of Magpie's bridle and Polly fetched the mounting block. Hayley climbed onto it and leaned across Magpie's back, then very gingerly lifted her feet so that her full weight was across the saddle. Magpie didn't budge. "Lead her round in a small circle, Sarah." Hayley instructed and Sarah did just that. Magpie didn't blink and so Hayley gentle swung her leg over the saddle and sat upright on her. Magpie was completely calm.

Polly checked the fitting and deciding that it was a bit too far down at the back, and went to her car to get another saddle. This procedure was repeated several times until the right saddle was found: a second hand, general purpose saddle. It was in very good condition and Sarah was delighted.

"Give her half an hour in the school, Sarah," suggested Hayley and she followed them back out to the arena to help Sarah mount Magpie for the very first time. It was so exciting, and when Sarah asked Magpie to trot, she found out what a difficult trot it was to rise to; it was much easier to sit to the trot instead of rising

"Gosh, I hope that she is going to be ok." Sarah called to Hayley, as she made her way around the outside of the school. Sitting to the trot, she bumped along like this until she got fed up with it and asked Magpie to canter. It was a lovely canter. "Thank goodness for that," thought Sarah.

* * *

Meanwhile, buried in the depths of Brecon, Jack was pretty happy with his arrangements. Stella was looking after him extremely well, but she didn't know what to do about the freeze mark she had found. She didn't want her money to have been spent in vain, and she didn't want to lose the horse that she had just bought for her Mother, even though she had bought him in good faith. She could ring the auctioneer: a stolen horse should be reported, but she was at a loss to get all her priorities in perspective. Stella knew she should ring the registry for freeze marks. She was perplexed, and just didn't know what to do. Jack was a nice horse. Her Mother had ridden him, once Stella had decided that he was safe, and she liked him very much. They had both become very fond of him, and christened him Chunky, because he was chunky. Just the sort of horse that Stella's Mother had been looking for. After a lengthy discussion, they decided that Stella should make her phone calls after the week end. She didn't like not knowing the truth.

* * *

Amber had been running for most of the night on Tuesday, trying to put as much distance between himself and that awful place. All day he wandered undiscovered in the Forest of Dean, occasionally spooked by the appearance of a wild boar, or the sudden explosion of a pheasant from the brambles that webbed across the untrodden areas of the forest floor. Nothing was familiar to him and he snatched grazing where he could find it, and wandered aimlessly through the night, to the following day. He wandered without direction for the remainder of the week, right up until Sunday morning. He had left the other horses far behind him and he knew not where they had got to, and cared not.

* * *

Steve and Lucy pulled up outside the address of the Bray brothers. They knocked the policeman's knock, on the front door of the farmhouse. The dwelling was run down and appeared semi-derelict. It looked as if it was the kind of front door that was only used for weddings and funerals. Gavin Bray cut a comical figure, appearing round the side of the house having come out of the back door. Half of his face was still covered in shaving foam and the braces to his twill trousers hung down around his knees. It was Saturday late afternoon, and he was getting ready to go out on the town with his brother. There was a darts tournament that they were taking part in and he was keen to scrub up clean and look his best. Madeline would be behind the bar that evening, and he liked Madeline.

"What can I do you for?" he asked, spitting shaving foam out onto the crazy paving in front of him. Steve announced who he was and why they were calling. Gavin confirmed that they had, indeed, bought some horses that week from the sale at Ross, pointing out that there was no law that said that they couldn't. Steve asked if he could see the horses and Gavin, being otherwise occupied, said that he would get his brother, and he disappeared. Steve and Lucy followed him, stepping gingerly, round the flotsam of dog poo that seemed to be everywhere in the garden - if you could call it a garden. Gavin invited them inside to the kitchen and the stench of human sweat, together with the smell of dogs, cats and general filth, was overpowering.

John was seated at the table. "Do you want a cup of tea?" he offered.

"No, we're good, thanks." Lucy replied quickly before Steve accepted, not that he was tempted. But it was unknown for him to turn down such an offer. Gavin returned to shaving over the kitchen sink, in among a motley collection of dirty dinner plates and other various crocks awaiting the attention of the scouring pad. Lucy mused that the crocks probably had a long wait.

"We'll get straight out there then," said John, and he led the way out into the yard. A large mangy dog pulled on the chain to get at them. Lucy was not sure if this was aggression or a plea for help. The yard was unkempt, with a plethora of redundant machinery, broken power tools and a whole variety of unidentifiable scrap scattered about in tangled heaps. They made the journey through the obstacle course, following John like sheep through the corrugated tin pig arks and broken sheep hurdles.

Lucy remarked on the difficulty of negotiating such a passageway and John laughed. "Farms are like that," he told her. "Scrap just breeds. You drop a couple of nuts and bolts on the ground and, in no time at all, you've got a pile of rusty old angle iron rods and a caravan chassis. I just don't know where it all comes from."

Lucy and Steve exchanged looks of bewilderment. Their glances were diverted as they rounded the corner and saw the five horses, who looked at them sorrowfully as they approached. They were the same horses that had followed Amber through the broken fence, but had been found on a triangle of common land, making good use of what grass had been available there. Gavin and John had wasted no time in rounding them up and returning them to a slightly better paddock, with wooden pallet fences in better order than the one they had escaped from. Lucy looked from one horse to the other, but nothing matched the description of Amber. "I believe you bought six horses, Mr Bray?" she asked. John considered the question. He knew it was an offence to allow a horse to wander, but they had caught these as soon as they had been reported, and no damage had been done. They could not find hide nor hair of the chestnut, so he considered that they could not be held responsible.

"Yeah," he replied finally, "that's right, we did. The whole lot escaped the night following the sale. We caught these, but one is still missing. If you find it, could you let us know, Missus. The bro' and me will be much obliged to you."

"The one you have missing, Mr Bray," Steve began, "we believe is stolen."

John was immediately defensive. "It weren't us who stole 'im. How was we to know, we bought 'em in good faiff, honest copper, we did."

"There is no suggestion of otherwise." Lucy was keen to keep them on side. "But if you hear of it turning up anywhere, perhaps you would let us know. Please, Mr Bray."

"What 'appens then, eh?" John was now seriously worried. They had paid good money for that horse and that could easily be money down the drain.

"I don't know," said Steve honestly. "It will become a dispute between you and the victim. The victim being the person who had the horse stolen."

"That's if it is the horse you are looking fer, Mister." John clutched at straws

"The first thing is to find the horse," Lucy said, "and the second thing is to catch the thief," she added. Then, after a thought, she continued; "You have been very helpful Mr Bray. Thank you for that." They shook hands and departed, leaving Gavin and John to their darts tournament.

* * *

The phone rang in the Mathew's household. It was Lucy, "Hello, Mum?" She began. "We've only just arrived back and we have gone straight to The Stewponey pub at Stourton." Lucy was ringing her parents from the pub foyer, just to let them know she was ok, and that she and Steve would be eating supper at the excellent carvery there. They had, after all, not seen her since she had left for work at 5.30 that morning.

"'Av yo' found them stolen 'osses?" asked Kate.

"I think we have found one of them, Mum."

"I'll tell Sarah. Her's bin that vexed."

Sarah looked up from her homework at the sound of her name. "Has she found them Mum?"

"Just one of them, Chook," Kate told her as she put the phone down.

"I wish I was old enough to join everyone in the Stewponey," Sarah grizzled.

* * *

Maisie was delighted to find them already settled in the public bar when she arrived. She was hungry, not only for some food, but also for the information she hoped that they had. "Oh, it is such a delight to see you two," she greeted them, pulling up a chair. They told her first how close they had come to finding Amber, and that the horse was believed to be loose somewhere in the Forest of Dean. "Oh my goodness," said Maisie clasping her face in her hands. "I can't believe he is loose, just wandering. Anything could happen to him. He might never get found; the forest is massive."

"We'll find him." Lucy caught Maisie's hand and gave it an encouraging squeeze, just as Hayley and Polly Purse came through the door. They were keen to get the lowdown on Steve and Lucy's trip. "I'm delighted you are here, too," said Lucy to Polly. "Are you going to Southall on Wednesday?"

"Yes, I'm there every week."

"You will be a good pair of eyes for us then," Steve was equally delighted. "I don't know yet if we can get there, but it will be good to know that you will be."

They continued to talk about the day's happenings. The dealers in Cinderford, and the address in Brecon, which they had yet to follow up on. They talked further about everything they knew, and listed the hard facts about this man with the distinctive horse box;

this man, who went by more than one name.

Maisie was champing at the bit to get her horses back. "We have the address where we think Jack might have gone to, don't we?" She said, seeing an opportunity of being able to assist in the enquiries. "I could go to that address at Brecon tomorrow, if I could find someone willing to take me" Maisie didn't have a car, just a push bike, and Brecon was a long way on one of those. She pondered further about whether she should bite the bullet and hire horse transport. She could see no reason why she couldn't just go and claim her horse back. But even then she did not want to go alone. It was a scary thing to do.

"The only person I know with transport for a horse, is Donna." Lucy mused tentatively, knowing that there had been bad blood between them.

"Would Donna come with me, do you think? Take me in her car and her horse trailer?" Maisie did sound desperate, and Lucy knew that Donna would, ordinarily, be the last person that Maisie would ask a favour of. But she couldn't see why not. Lucy saw kindness in Donna and thought that it was worth asking. She was going to offer to do it for her, but she considered that it would be better if Maisie asked her directly. Donna would admire that, hard though it would be for Maisie.

"You will have to pluck up the courage to ask her yourself, though," Lucy told her and, to her surprise, Maisie jumped to her feet, saying that there was no time like the present, and she disappeared out to the pub phone in the foyer. Donna answered the phone. She had been busy with clearing the supper dishes off the table when it rung. Maisie took a deep breath in as she heard the ringing tone at the other end, "Hello, Donna? I am sorry to take you by surprise but this is Maisie. I hope you don't mind me ringing you."

"Maisie? Good heavens! Yes, you're right, I am surprised. What can I do for you?" Donna was on her guard rather, but she had heard of Maisie's horses being stolen and she would not wish that on anyone. When Maisie finally got around to explaining why she had rung, Donna said that she would be glad to help her recover her horses.

Maisie returned a few minutes later, very pleased with the conversation she had just had. "Yes, she says that she can help. I am meeting her at the stables tomorrow at nine o'clock." Maisie was just so excited.

Lucy said that she could ask to have a policeman from the South Wales Police go with them in the morning, and inform the buyers that they were in possession of a stolen horse. She suggested that this would be more official and put them on the 'back-foot,' so to speak. If Maisie took with her all the freeze mark documentary evidence she had, then there would be no denying that she had a valid claim on Jack. Maisie agreed with this and promised to dig out everything that she had. The evening finished full of hope and anticipation, as they retired to their respective homes, to sleep fitfully in preparation.

* * *

When Steve and Lucy arrived at work for early turn, on that Sunday morning, Steve rang Brecon police. "Heddlu Aberhonddu," spoke a voice with an extremely Welsh accent down the phone. "Alla i eich helpu chi?"

"Pardon me?" Steve didn't speak Welsh.

"Brecon Police, can I help you?" The voice repeated in English, and Steve explained what had happened and everything that he knew. The good man of the Welsh Constabulary told him what he should do. "Come to the police station first," he suggested, and one of us will go with them to Coulter Close. So long as Maisie can prove ownership, there should be no problem. Steve then rang Donna, catching her just before she left for the stables with her trailer, and told her what had been suggested.

"That sounds like a good plan," she agreed, thinking that having the strong arm of the law on your side would always be a plus. She and the children arrived at Chestnut Farm before any of the others, and this gave her the chance of checking round on a few things. The end of the month had come and Donna had to prepare their invoices for the rent money. Any hay and straw that was used was all administered on trust. When the girls had to open a new large bale of hay, or help themselves to straw, they wrote it on the blackboard in the tea room, and Donna would then know how much to add to their bill.

Maisie freewheeled into the yard in good time for their trip south. She did feel a little awkward, this being the first time she would come face to face with Donna since her heated departure two years ago. But Donna was good at putting people at their ease, and greeted her warmly, saying that it was good to have her back as a friend.

* * *

Sarah was keen to ride her new horse now that she was all kitted out. She would have liked to be in on the excitement with the grown-ups but, on balance, Magpie was a much more exciting challenge. Hayley was also looking forward to a Sunday ride over Kinver Edge on Tambourine. Donna's children, Carol and Michael, were going to go with their Mother to Brecon, but when they realised that Hayley and Sarah were planning a long ride, they changed their minds. "Can't we stay with Hayley and Sarah, Mum?" they had pleaded. Donna hesitated. It wasn't that she didn't trust them or Hayley, but she would be a long way away if there was a problem. Peter had gone off to play a round of golf, but she considered that Hayley could get hold of him easily enough if she needed to.

"Yes alright, you can stay," Donna agreed. "If that is ok with Hayley." And Hayley said that she would be delighted to have them along: the more the merrier she said, adding that Gill would be riding with them too.

"I can take them all for lunch," she added. "We can go to The Anchor in Caunsall. I always look forward to one of their excellent filled rolls and there will be plenty of salad. They won't starve Donna, I promise."

Donna gave Hayley some money to cover the cost of lunch for

the children, and they waved goodbye, heading south for the M5. Sarah had already made a start with Magpie, getting her ready and giving her a good groom. Carol, Michael and Gill dashed off to the pony paddock to bring in all three ponies, Mouse, Helen and Moony. Radar and Tetley chased after them and told the ponies off for breathing. They certainly would have been easier to catch if the terriers hadn't been involved, but a carrot or two goes a long way in the remit of a pony's priorities. They looked a motley bunch tied up in a row on the yard, with their muddy legs and skids of earth stuck to their cheeks where they had laid in the mud and rested their pretty little heads in places where they should not have laid them.

"I do hope Maisie gets her horses back today," said Sarah, as they waved them goodbye.

Chapter Seven
On The Edge

As soon as Sarah had her feet in the stirrups of Magpie's new saddle, her butterflies subsided. She had been as excited as a toddler at the prospect of going on a hack with her very own horse. She patted Magpie's neck and ran her hand inside the locks of her mane, feeling the warmth seeping through her soft winter coat. Magpie stood quietly watching the others get ready for the ride. Hayley was helping the others climb aboard their ponies. She was helping Michael anyway, because Mouse was never that good at standing still while she was being mounted. Gill and Carol were full of chatter as they clambered into their saddles, Carol on Helen, and Gill on Moony. Radar and Tetley sat and waited, full of anticipation that they might be invited along too. Lucy did take them with her often when she rode out on Cosmo, and Hayley had frequently been with her, so she knew she could rely on the dogs to behave, especially on the road. It didn't take much for Hayley to be persuaded by Sarah that they could come along.

When they reached the gate to the road, Hayley instructed them all to stop and look to see if there was any traffic coming.

"We know there are no cars, Hayley," Michael squeaked. "I don't see why we have to do this."

"One of the days," Hayley explained, for the umpteenth time, "you may need your pony to stop in a hurry, and if she is not used to doing that, then you might find it difficult and you could have an accident." Michael pulled a face and the girls laughed at him, pointing and wagging their fingers.

Single file, they set off down the lane and over the canal towards Kinver Edge. At the end of Windsor Holloway, they turned left towards Cookley, then right into Gypsy Lane, where there were some horses grazing in the fields by the road. They flew about in an excited frenzy when the Chestnut Farm horses passed by, bucking and breaking wind, with their winter rugs of various colours, flapping and jangling amid the high jinks. Magpie broke into a trot, a high stepping trot that made the children laugh.

"That's amazing," said Carol, "however does she manage to do that?"

"She just does it," said Sarah. "You can't rise to it, you have to sit. It's not ideal but her canter is lovely." The terriers trotted confidently in front of the caravan of children, which was a good place for them to be because Hayley could keep an eye on them, to make sure they behaved themselves.

At the end of the lane, down through the rock cutting, they saw Kinver Edge in front of them at long last. Once through the picnic area and car park, there was the chance for a blast of speed, and the five of them flew up the sandy track to the top followed by Radar and Tetley who lacked the speed of the horses. Kinver Edge is a long beautiful ridgeway with spectacular views in all directions. There are the Welsh mountains to the West, Shropshire to the North, the Malvern Hills to the South and Birmingham to the East, with the high rise apartments in Dudley and the puffing chimneys of the glass industry in Stourbridge. Sarah had walked up there many times, but to see it from the back of a horse was just the best. As they walked along the ridgeway, Sarah looked down the steep slope on their right. There was a track down the other side of the Edge, and Hayley suggested that they take that path. Sarah said that she would prefer not to until she was more confident with Magpie. She would play it safe and leave that steep track for another day. Hayley agreed that this was probably the sensible thing to do.

They knew that halfway down the steep slope there were the old rock houses. Many times in the past, they had all scrambled down to look at them and play games. You could explore the caves and imagine how life must have been like for the cave dwellers. Dug out of the sandstone rock, these were a well-kept secret in the West Midlands, created in the eighteenth century by itinerant labourers coming to the area to dig out the canal system. Desperate for shelter in which to house their families, they dug caves out of the soft sandstone rock, making their homes in the escarpment. The living was agreeable and they put down roots, generation after generation, and so these rock houses were occupied by their descendants into the nineteen-fifties.

Sarah sighed with contentment and Hayley glanced round to look at her. She smiled, knowing exactly how lovely it was to be up there on your own horse. She gave Tambourine an affectionate pat on the shoulder. "You could be anywhere in the country here," she said. "This always reminds me of the Brecon Beacons; you are just so high up. This is fabulous riding."

"Mum and Maisie are in the Brecon Beacons now." Michael piped up, and their thoughts were simultaneously now focused on wondering how Donna and Maisie were getting on with their search for Jack and Amber.

* * *

Constable Jones, or Jones the Law, as his neighbours at home called him, knocked purposefully, as all policemen do, on the door of 'The Oaks'. Stella's Mother was not that surprised to see them standing there: one policeman and two ladies, with a car and horse trailer parked out on the road. She knew straight away why they had called. "You had better come in," she invited them. "STELLA!" she called to her daughter, "You'd better come downstairs, the Heddlu are here."

Stella and her Mother were dismayed at the visit, but knew that co-operation was the best way forward, and they could only imagine the distress that Maisie must have been in. Donna, Maisie, and Jones the Law all made themselves comfortable at the kitchen table while Stella's Mother prepared a brew of tea. "We bought him in good faith, I won't lie to you" explained Stella," and we have become very fond of Chunky. He is a nice horse."

"Chunky?" exclaimed Maisie, "Yeah, you could describe him as chunky, I suppose."

"What is his name?" asked Stella.

"Jack." Maisie replied.

"Oh!" Stella was disappointed. "I was expecting something more exciting than Jack." She suddenly realised how rude that must sound. "I am sorry, I didn't mean to offend you."

Maisie laughed. "It is short for Stonewall Jackson. No doubt you can see why."

"The American Confederate General!" Stella's Mother looked back at them from her teapot duties.

"I think it has more to do with what he would knock down if you tried to stop him." Donna laughed. They all laughed, even Jones the Law.

Maisie did appreciate that they could not possibly have known that Jack was hot property, and this was as big a tragedy for her too. "Look," said Maisie, "We are both losers in this one, but I would happily pay a reward for the safe return of both my horses. I will meet you half way on what you paid for him." Then, as an afterthought she asked, "What did you pay?"

"Two hundred and twenty-five guineas," Stella replied dolefully. And Maisie asked her if she thought that her offer was fair. Stella and her Mother thought that it was more than fair, even though this was a hard lesson to learn. Maisie rummaged in her purse. "Excuse the moths," she said jovially. They went to get Jack, and Maisie was quite envious of their set up. It was a big house, stables and paddocks at the end of the garden. Jack must have felt that he had landed on his feet.

"I would like to know if you find Amber," Stella told them, as they led Jack up into Donna's trailer.

"I can't believe that he will stay undetected forever," Donna reassured the girls, and she glanced at Jones the Law for confirmation, but he was speaking on his personal radio. It transpired that there had been a rather fortunate development.

* * *

Back in the home beat office in Stourbridge, Lucy answered the phone. "Home Beat Office, WPC Mathews speaking. Can I help you?" The call had been put through to her from the front office and the caller was young Lewis Lewis, the sheep farmer they had met at Ross-on-Wye. Lewis the Sheep, his friends called him with no character analysis intended.

"Grazing in Lydney Park, he was," said Lewis, reporting that Amber had been found. "I had put the word about like you said I should, and my mate rang me this morning."

Lucy was just thrilled to bits that the last piece of the jigsaw puzzle had been put into place, and she immediately rang Brecon police. They in turn contacted Jones the Law, who wasted no time in telling Maisie and Donna the good news.

"How far away is the horse?" asked Donna, thinking that if it was not too far, they could collect him on the way home.

"Your horse, Amber, is safely installed at Two Brookes Farm," Jones the Law told them and, after consulting a map, Donna said that they could go there and collect him straight away.

Maisie was beside herself. She never thought that she would get both of her horses back and in the same day. A couple of days ago she thought that she would never see either of them ever again. Stella and her Mother were delighted for them too, and they made a resolution to stay in touch. In any case, they believed that if they could track down the horse thief, they might both get their money back. If new friends had been made, then some good had come out of all this mess. They all agreed it was going to be ok.

* * *

When the five ponies, their riders and their dogs reached the end of The Edge, they took the right hand pathway that led down to the other side, as it was a gentler slope than the other path. At the bottom they turned right where there were more picnic areas and open spaces. Some boys had cobbled together a game of cricket, and folks were walking their dogs. Radar and Tetley ventured to make friends with a yellow Labrador and Sarah shouted to them:

"This way boys, leave her alone."

The cricketing boys, being boys, shouted out some rude words to them which Hayley ignored. "Get off your horse and milk it!" one of them yelled, and Carol, Sarah and Gill all stuck their tongues out. Michael thought that these older boys were really cool, and were not in any way directing their comments towards him, so he just grinned at them in a 'I'm one of you, all blokes together' kind of a way.

They had another lovely canter along a sandy track until they came to Kingsford Lane, which they had to join to loop back towards home. For a two lane backwater, the road was surprisingly busy. It was a bit concerning for Hayley to have the terriers loose on the lane, but all the horses were proving to be remarkably well behaved. A big Rottweiler dog threw itself at the fence on the opposite side of the road, barking as they passed by. Radar and Tetley hugged the nearside kerb looking apprehensively at the direction of the noise. "It's ok boys, on you go," Sarah told them encouragingly. Moony jogged a little and Tambourine gave it a bit of a look, but Magpie remained calm and steady. Sarah and Hayley were more than impressed with her. She really was a lovely little horse they agreed.

The girls were looking forward to another long canter up the sandy track to Blakeshall. It had been an exhilarating ride so far, and, being uphill, Hayley felt it appropriate to let Tambourine go at a faster pace and so she 'opened her up.' The sound of her foot falls hammered underneath her as she went lickety-split, chucking gravelly sand in her wake. Magpie tried to keep up but she didn't have the same speed, and Gill on Moony came alongside. The girls grinned at each other in their mutual enjoyment and, in that split second lapse of concentration, they did not see the pot-bellied pig come grunting out of the undergrowth right in front of Hayley and Tambourine.

Tambourine jinked to one side and Hayley struggled to stay in the saddle as the little lemon and white skewbald went into fourth gear, disappearing out of sight round the bend up the track. Magpie threw out the anchors and slid to an abrupt stop, as Moony tried hard to do the same but Magpie inadvertently bumped her, and Gill fell forward and slid unceremoniously down her shoulder and onto the muddy track. She gamely hung on to the reins so Moony was unable to tank off after Hayley and Tambourine. The terriers were right in the wake of the horse's hooves and lost no time in plastering Gill's face with doggy licks as she lay crumpled in the mud. Helen piled into the back of Magpie, and Mouse piled into the back of Helen. It was a right royal collision with tiny dogs in the centre of the affray. Gill got quickly to her feet pushing Radar and Tetley out of harm's way before the shuffling ponies stood on her or them. "Are you ok, Gill?" asked Michael.

"Yes," Gill replied, her bottom lip beginning to wobble. She fought to keep her composure, hiding her face as tears began to well up. "I'm just a bit muddy."

Sarah's eyes were still on the pig and she was wondering what it was going to do next. The dogs were thinking the same thing. The pig, however, a black one, was totally unaware of the chaos it had just caused and looked dolefully at them, probably wondering what strange game they were playing. Another pig came rootling through the undergrowth to join it, and then another. The ponies, apart from Magpie, instinctively took a few paces backwards as three pigs looked at the riders and the riders looked at the pigs. Tetley's expressive ears shot up, and Radar hid behind him trying to look brave. Gill clambered back onto Moony, breathing deeply as her loss of pride subsided. Sarah held the pony for her, and they considered what they were going to do. Hayley was nowhere to be seen.

Michael felt that he should take charge, being the man, and pushed his way forward on Mouse and started to shout at the pigs. "Go away, you rotten pigs!" he yelled at them and the pigs took not one bit of notice, but the terriers knew just what to do and barked furiously in support. Sarah felt that Michael needed help, so she rode alongside him and joined in the shouting. Magpie and Mouse were very brave not to swerve away from animals that horses are traditionally scared of; but how was Sarah to know that Magpie had been bought up with pigs, and couldn't see what all the fuss was about.

Gill joined forces on Moony, and Carol urged Helen to fall in the ranks. The ponies' courage was strengthened because Magpie set such a good example. Four of them in a row, filling the track, amid the noise of the terriers. They moved forward, step by step, with the children shouting. Radar and Tetley piled in nipping the pigs on the ankles. The pigs didn't like this one little bit and squeaked, turning to bite the dogs. The brave little dogs were undeterred and nipped back fiercely, until the pigs decided that this entertainment had lost its attraction, and they had better things to attend to in the undergrowth further into the woods.

Hayley could hear the shouting and the barking as she returned. Tambourine had taken off in a full-blown bolt when she had caught sight of the pigs coming through the undergrowth. Hayley had no idea what had spooked her horse, thinking more about staying on board than looking behind her. She had the most awful trouble pulling Tambourine up to a walk, but pull her up she did, and now she was heading back to where she had parted company with the rest of the gang. She rounded the corner in the track and was very amused to see four ponies in a line, plus canine back-up, fending off the pigs. "Oh my goodness me," she exclaimed, and couldn't help laughing at the spectacle.

So, in the end, there was no harm done, and the remainder of the ride was uneventful. Riding past the sawmill with its whirling machinery, they left The Edge behind them and rode in single file along Gypsy Lane, back to Windsor Holloway.

* * *

"There shouldn't be pigs on Kinver Edge," said Carol tucking into her ham cob at The Anchor in Caunsall.

"No, there shouldn't," said Sarah.

"I have heard," began Hayley, "these pigs have become really fashionable, and are being released into the wild all over the country when their owners get fed up with them. I have heard of some stories where they have really caused big problems."

"What sort of problems?" asked Gill.

"You should know," Michael piped up. "You were the one that fell off."

"I didn't fall off," Gill was indignant. "I dismounted."

"Without permission," said Carol.

"It was a clumsy hang-on at best," Michael chirped as he took another mouthful of his ham roll.

"People take them on as piglets, thinking that they are so cute," Hayley continued, "then they grow up, and become a thorough nuisance."

"They don't call them pot-bellied pigs for nothing do they?" Michael surfaced from his ham roll.

"They house-train them, don't they?" Sarah asked.

"Indeed they do," Hayley replied. "Like you would want to have a pig in the house! Ugly things, and they are a nightmare in the garden."

"I wonder which one lives in the straw house," Michael asked. The girls looked at him bewildered. "One of them lives in a straw house, one lives in a house made of sticks and one lives in a brick built house," he explained.

"Of course, they do," Carol smiled at her little brother. "But I don't think we'll ever know the answer to that."

"If I was the Big Bad Wolf, I'd soon find out." Michael had to content himself with that happy thought.

"We've got two big bad wolves right here." Sarah bent down under the table to fuss the terriers, who were busy hoovering the carpet of fallen crumbs.

"So, people just get rid of them when they're fed up with them digging the garden and coming in the house with muddy feet?" asked Gill. "That's dreadful. The poor pigs. They are just turned loose to fend for themselves."

"Yep. They looked to be doing alright, though, didn't they?" Sarah laughed.

* * *

Meanwhile, Donna's Range Rover and trailer rolled down the bumpy track to Maisie's stables with Jack and Amber. Their differences seemed a world away now as their friendship re-established itself, and they settled both the horses in the paddock with some hay. Donna headed back to Chestnut Farm where she found a very muddy child with a story to tell. They were so excited to tell their Mother all about it, saying that they were going to ride their ponies every day during the coming half term, to see if they could find some more pigs.

Chapter Eight
Half Term Holidays

These were happy days. These were the half term holidays, and Sarah had her very own pony to share them with. She was blissfully happy, living the dream she had been cherishing for many years.

The yard was a hive of activity on Sunday morning. Donna's children, Michael and Carol, were in a spin getting their ponies ready for the big day: the Half Term Fun Day at the Riding School for Children in Stourton. Gill arrived early, armed with her outfit for the fancy dress. She was going as an Indian squaw and her pony, Moony, would make a good companion with her blanket spot appaloosa markings. She was confident that she would win.

Michael was going as Darth Vader, dressed in black with a mask that Donna had made for him out of four squares of shiny black card. The detail had been picked out in white strips stuck on with glue. Michael's pony, Mouse, was going as herself, having no firm thoughts about Star Wars.

Sarah was going as a fairy, dressed in black and white to match Magpie's colouring. It was an unusual choice but very effective. Michael sang a teasing song at her: "I'm a fairy, my name's Nuff."

"Fair enough," Gill and Carol finished the well-worn verse.

"Fairy Nuff?" Hayley tutted and flicked her chin up at the children, disappearing into Tambourine's stable. Carol had decided to go as Little Red Riding Hood, with Helen as the wolf. Donna had made a head cover for Helen out of tan coloured fur fabric, to match the rest of her. She gave the wolf's head a snarly face with white felt triangles for teeth. Carol was busy binding up Helen's tail so that it looked more like a wolf's tail than a pony's.

A frenzy of excitement enveloped the stables that morning. They not only had the fancy dress to look forward to, but there would be gymkhana classes and clear round jumping. Hayley agreed to go and watch them for part of the day and, if Lucy finished work on time, she might get there for the fancy dress. "Are you going to come and join us?" she had asked Steve, but he said that he would rather watch the grass growing. Lucy gave him an affectionate shove. "What will you be like when you are a dad?" she teased.

"That's a long way off," replied Steve and Lucy sighed a sigh of resignation, thinking that it needn't be. She really did love Steve.

The indoor school at Stourton Riding School for Children was big and airy. There were loads of other children there from all around the area. Proud grandparents had also come along to join the fun. They all jumped up and down enthusiastically when the relay race of four teams of rowdy children competed in the bending poles for first place. Then again, they cheered when they hurtled down the school aiming for the finish line with eggs on spoons, dragging their ponies behind them. Sarah and Magpie won a first rosette for that race, and Sarah beamed at her big sister seated in the gallery, earlier than expected from work. Last but not least came the fancy dress, and Carol caught the judges' eye in her Little Red Riding Hood costume. Then, still in their fancy dress outfits, all the children went out on a short hack down the bridle path and back along Hyde Lane. It had been a really lovely day, and the children hugged themselves with pleasure in their beds that night. All lost inside their memories of the day's fun and games.

* * *

Later in the week, Lucy and Sarah needed some more carrots for Cosmo and Magpie, so they set off up the road to Horses Galore. Polly was in fine form when they arrived in the shop, which was as busy as you would expect for half term. Polly found time to catch up on news with Lucy, while Sarah looked at some snazzy coloured riding tops and some knickers, designed especially for riding horses. Even though it had been a couple of weeks since the theft of Maisie's horses, the topic was still current. "That was a close call," Polly said.

"It's a good job that Steve and I were on the case so quickly," confessed Lucy proudly. "Though I say it myself, we were interested enough to put ourselves out."

"Have you got enough evidence to prosecute that thief?"

"No, I don't think we have. I keep saying that we should apply for a warrant to arrest him and then, once we get him in a police cell, we can use the thumbscrews to extract a confession."

"Oh Lucy! You are so naughty. You can't do that." Polly laughed, knowing her friend was joking.

"No, we can't, sadly." Lucy grinned back at Polly, "but I can dream." Polly talked about her visit to Southall Market that week. She talked about the colourful characters, some she liked and some she didn't; some of the dealers she would trust and some she wouldn't. She talked about the flashing of horses down the High Street with all the excitement of a Middle Eastern bazaar. It was made more colourful by the Asian shops spilling onto the pavements with their varied and cosmopolitan products, and the buzzing of the shoppers in their vibrant turbans and their beautiful flowing saris. All this made the High Street narrower than it should be. Add fast trotting horses, with the entourage of interested buyers shouting their enthusiasm, and the Bobbies were soon spilling out of the police station opposite. Their attempts to bring normality back from the mayhem was always finite, but only after arrests had been made.

"This did not always suit Jim Bannister," Polly added, reminding Lucy that he was the equestrian sleuth from the Metropolitan Police Mounted Branch that she had mentioned before. "Sometimes it disrupted his investigations, and had an adverse effect on how the police were perceived by the horse dealers, who, for the most part, co-operated with Jim when he interviewed them. He is a respected figure by both sides," Polly told Lucy, "Eye candy too," she added with a twinkle. "He is known by his colleagues as the Peeler Dealer. He mingles so well with the market fraternity."

"Can I get Magpie a spare lead rope please, Lucy." Sarah asked.

"What do you want a spare for?"

"Look at this sparkly black one, it's so pretty." Sarah put her case.

"Yes ok, if it makes you happy." And Lucy turned back to Polly to continue their conversation. She was fascinated by all of this and wished that there was a weekly horse market in the West Midlands where she could hone her own investigative talents. "I am going to have to visit this Southall Market some time," she said. "It sounds so exciting, Polly."

"Come down there with me one week, when you have the day off on a Wednesday." Polly suggested. "There is no reason why you shouldn't. There is a chuck wagon there, selling the best jellied eels in the country, as well as excellent fish and chips."

"Jellied eels!" Lucy exclaimed. "Urgh!"

"Don't knock them till you have tried them, Lucy." Polly laughed. "Let me know when you have a Wednesday off duty and we will go down together. It will be fun."

"That's a date," said Lucy as she left the shop. "Tara a bit."

* * *

Steve was waiting for them when they got back to the stables and had the kettle on ready. Lucy couldn't wait to tell him of her plans of going to Southall with Polly, and this reminded him of how disgruntled he was for letting a horse thief slip through his fingers. "He will not slip away so easily next time," he told the girls. "Not if I have anything to do with it anyway."

"Of course not, Steve," Lucy said patting him on the head like he was an obedient dog.

Like any sunny springtime day, the air was full of hope and expectation. Sarah was thoroughly enjoying her new horse, getting to know her and finding out all her little foibles. Magpie didn't like to eat her hay out of a hay net; she preferred to nose it around on the floor, and so that's where Sarah put it. As far as she was concerned, Magpie could have whatever she wanted. She was a bit bewildered with her, though, when she chucked her bucket feed onto the floor as well. Sarah could not work out how she did this, because the bucket stayed firmly in its bracket. She decided to watch her while she was eating, and was amazed to see what she did.

Magpie would trap a handful of her feed between the side of her muzzle and the side of the bucket, then she would slide it up to the top of the bucket and whizz it out. Why did she do that? Nobody knew. It seemed to be just a game she played while she was munching each mouthful. It wasn't that she did not want her food, as she was keen as mustard when feeding time came. Sarah puzzled over how she could solve this problem. The food that Magpie whizzed out just fell into the straw bed and got wasted.

She tried giving her a bigger bucket so that she could sift it around better without spilling any. Horses are known for wanting to eat from the bottom of the manger, so a larger bucket would allow them to do this. But that didn't work. She thought of keeping the front of the stable clear of bedding, and sweep it clean so that Magpie could pick up her dropped food from the floor afterwards. It worked to a point, but was not the best solution. Then Lucy had a brainwave. She took Sarah to Horses Galore and they bought two big buckets, one slightly bigger than the other. Steve cut the bottom out of the smaller one for them, and drilled holes round the top of both buckets. He secured them together with baler twine, the smaller one going inside the larger one. Then, to stop them from being moved around the stable, Steve anchored them to one of the inside timbers with a loop of baler twine and a quick release knot.

Magpie had to put her head through the small bucket and retrieve her food from the bottom of the big one, then, when she tried to slide a handful of the feed up the side of the bucket, it caught on the cut edge of the smaller bucket and fell back where it had come from. Magpie ate all of her feed and there was not a grain spilled. Sarah was very pleased with their efforts and proudly showed Hayley, who was equally impressed.

* * *

On the last day of half term, Lucy and Sarah were planning to go on a nice long ride. Hayley had Magpie, Tambourine and Cosmo all tacked up and ready to go when they arrived that morning, and they lost no time in grabbing their hats from the tea room, and were out onto the lane, with Magpie and the terriers leading the way. Hayley called Sarah back, and reminded her that it is always a good idea to insist that the horses stopped and waited for a few seconds, before entering the lane.

"Tell me why do we do that again?" Sarah asked her, not having concentrated the last time she had been told.

"The cars come so fast down this lane," Hayley explained patiently. "If the horses are used to stopping here then, when you really need them to stop, they know what to do." Sarah nodded, understanding the logic. Lucy suggested giving a verbal command as well as pulling on the reins and flexing the buttocks.

"What sort of command?" Sarah asked, and Lucy suggested one. "Heave down the anchor, me hearty."

Hayley laughed. "Idiot," she looked sideways at Lucy. "Just say 'Whoa,' Sarah" They completed the little exercise before joining the terriers who had been waiting patiently.

A colourful narrowboat was gliding under the bridge in Windsor Holloway as they rode over, and Magpie sidestepped away from it, turning her head to have a better look. But that was all she did. She was such an honest and trustful little horse, and Sarah gave her a hearty pat of approval. They waved at the jolly boatman steering his vessel from the rear of the boat. "You are on the move early in the year," called Lucy to him, and he replied that he didn't want to waste a day of sunshine. The summer was way too short as it was, he added.

That afternoon, they went right the way over to Shatterford. Sarah was getting to know all the bridleways in the area, and learning the different routes she could take over The Edge. Learning all about Magpie and her funny little ways every day was a pleasure. She practiced bringing her to a halt in all sorts of different places after that, and Magpie became very responsive to the verbal commands that Sarah gave her.

"It has been an amazing week," said Sarah to her Mum and Dad, hugging herself with the pleasure of being alive, and having such lovely friends, such a lovely sister, and a lovely pony. "They will be green with envy when I tell the rest of my class what I've been up to this half term."

Practical Kate reminded Sarah of the homework she had been given. "Ay it doon, Sarah?" she asked. Sarah's bubble popped, and she confessed that it was mostly done, and that would do. "I aye tellin' yo agen Bab, yam back at skewall tomorrow. Yode best get it doon." Sarah pulled a face.

Chapter Nine
Three Little Pigs

Sarah loved going to Chestnut Farm after school every evening, getting the stable ready and bringing Magpie into the warm and putting on her stable rug. It was a modern synthetic lightweight rug, so much easier to handle than the more usual, heavy jute rugs. Magpie wore a waterproof New Zealand rug in the field during the day so, when it was time to ride her, the bulk of her body was already mud free. The winter coat was starting to drop as the weather warmed and Sarah couldn't wait for the summer coat to be through properly. "I bet she will really shine then," she told Lucy.

Their long hacks over The Edge at the weekends were pleasant and uneventful until one Saturday, when they were just crossing the glade where the boys played games of cricket and football. There was the sound of clattering hooves on Drakelow Lane, and the girls instinctively looked round towards the noise, just as a large bay thoroughbred horse burst through the bushes, startling the terriers who kicked off, barking at it, so that the horse turned on its fetlocks and headed up the track that they had just come down.

Some boys were just arriving to play cricket, laden down with their willow bats and armfuls of wicket stumps. The horse spotted them blocking his path and skidded to a halt, considered his options for a moment, before spinning back towards the clearing.

The girls had been stopped in their tracks and were stationary in a huddle when the horse returned. Lucy called to it in a calming voice. "It's all right, whoa there, feller, whoooa, whoooa." she cooed to it. He stopped, feet planted firmly as if ready for a second take off. Letting out a loud snort his tense muscular form softened slightly as he began to let down his guard. He was a herd animal, just like the Chestnut Farm horses, and his safety lay in staying in their company.

Magpie snorted back, "Hey you!" Sarah poked her on the neck, "Don't you go causing trouble."

Lucy pushed Cosmo towards him but he was wary of being caught and kept a distance between them. Hayley, on Tambourine, also attempted to catch hold of his reins without success. The young cricketers arrived in the clearing and watched the proceedings silently. One of them approached the horse with caution and, with an offering of a handful of grass he had grabbed from the side of the path, he was able to reach the dangling reins. On realising he was captured, the horse pulled back but the lad was a game little chap and hung on tightly till the thoroughbred relaxed and stood still.

Lucy jumped to the ground and, handing Cosmo's reins for Sarah to hold, she took the horse from the boy and thanked him heartily.

"What are we going to do now?" She asked the other two.

"There must be a rider somewhere." Hayley stated the obvious. "The horse came from the bridle path across the road, I shouldn't wonder."

"What ever frightened him?" Sarah asked.

"We'll probably never know." Lucy was more concerned with what they were going to do with him now. If no one appeared to claim him soon, they would have to take him with them back to Chestnut Farm. That really was too far to lead a large unpredictable horse. The lanes could be dangerous at the weekends, with boy racers out for a joy ride and dog walkers cluttering the Queen's Highway. It was hard enough having the dogs to look out for.

"I know a man who lives in a house along here," Hayley volunteered. "He's a friend of Dave's. I think he has a bit of land at the back. I wonder if he would keep the horse there till we can find his owner."

"Anything's worth a try," said Lucy. "Sarah, give Cosmopolitan Lady to Hayley. You can't ride and lead when we get to the road, it's too dangerous." So, with Lucy walking with this spirited giant of a horse, Hayley and Cosmo led the way behind the terriers who trotted happily in front, and Sarah rode Magpie at the rear of the procession, keeping on The Edge before going over a shallow ditch, and crossing the road to the safety of Dave's friend, Mr Nix.

The bungalow was surrounded by manicured lawns, decorated with an array of horse drawn implements complementing the neat flower beds. Lucy couldn't see how this was going to work. Sarah jumped off and rang the bell from the end of Magpie's reins. Mr Nix came to the door. "Hello," Sarah said, not knowing what to say next.

"Hello, Mr Nix," Hayley called from behind the gathering of horses and dogs. Taking over the conversation, she explained what had happened.

"Running loose, you say?" Mr Nix was as bewildered as they were. "Someone will be lying injured somewhere," he suggested, and this would not do. "Those dratted pigs," he spat out his deduction of the situation. "I bet it's those dratted pigs. They've jumped out of the bushes and frightened this poor horse to death."

"We are no strangers to that happening," Hayley told him. Sarah smiled to herself. Now that the drama was history, it was quite funny to recall. "I cannot tell you how often I have chased them out of my garden."

"Oh my goodness," said Lucy. "That must have been terrible for you. You keep it all lovely"

"They are not welcome here, that's for sure."

Mrs Nix came to the door when she heard Hayley's voice. "Hello, Mrs Nix," Hayley greeted her fondly.

"Yes, of course you can put him in our paddock," she told them. "You know we have a pony out there, so he'll been safe next to her"

"Those pigs have scared that old pony to bits, although, I have to say, she takes no notice of them now," Mr Nix told them. "Dolly was my daughter's pony. We've never had the heart to sell her. But never mind that, let me take him from you and I'll park him next to Dolly in the paddock. Do you want to leave your little dogs here, too?"

"Oh, yes please," said Lucy who was starting to think that coming out with two dogs on the loose was not such a good idea at the weekend.

The girls thanked him kindly and, having seen the horse settled next to Dolly, they set out to retrace their steps and backtrack where they thought the horse had come from. Lucy rode back through the rough ground on The Edge, to where they had been riding. Hayley and Sarah followed the road as far as the point where they thought that the horse had crossed over. They turned left onto the bridle path in the direction of Shatterford, having to ride single file because it was so narrow. Hayley was in front, and scanned what she could see of the path ahead as it looped around a rather splendid garden with a pretty little brook running through it.

"I'm going to live in a house like that," said Sarah, from the rear.

"Are you indeed," replied the elder sister. "Let me know and I'll move in with you."

"We could all live together," Sarah voiced her wish list, "You, me and Steve."

"Ooh Steve too, is it?" Lucy laughed.

"Are you going to marry Steve?" asked Sarah out of the blue.

Lucy didn't know. She fell silent, locked momentarily in her own thoughts, before volunteering an answer. "He hasn't asked me."

"Will you say yes if he does?"

"Sarah! For goodness sake, I don't know. Probably. Who knows what the future holds."

"If I tell him that you will, he might feel more inclined to ask."

"SARAH! Don't you dare. Don't you dare say a word to Steve. This is between me and him. Don't you go meddling!"

Hayley giggled at the conversation she was privy to, thinking quietly that she was glad she didn't have a younger sister. As they rounded the next corner, they saw a figure up ahead, hurrying towards them. The jodhpurs and long riding boots she was wearing, gave them every reason to believe that they had found the casualty.

"Have you seen a loose horse on your travels?" the girl shouted ahead to them, as she broke into a run.

"Yes we have," they all chorused together. "He's quite safe," Hayley told her, "he's parked at a friend's house just along the road. It's not far."

"Is he alright?" The girl was bent double as she spoke, with her head between her knees, and she noisily heaved in breaths of air. She had walked and run a long way and was now feeling the effects.

"He looked fine," said Hayley, "if a little wound up. Take your time, you sound puffed out."

"I've got a stitch" the girl said, "I haven't had one of those for years." She heaved some more breath into her lungs. "I'll be alright in a minute."

"Are you ok?" Lucy asked her, her first-aiding skills coming to the fore.

"Other than the stitch? Yes, I'm fine, thank you." And the girl straightened up holding her sides. "I'm Petra," she volunteered her identity, and they all introduced themselves. Lucy said that as soon as she was able, they would take her to where her horse was waiting.

* * *

Dolly was enjoying the company of another horse, and they were grooming each other over the fence when the girls arrived back at the Nix's bungalow. "He must have been heading home," Petra concluded.

Mrs Nix offered everyone a cup of tea before they departed. "Would your horses go out in the paddock, too?" she asked. They reasoned that as they had led the horse some distance, and as they had not reacted badly to each other, they would probably be ok. They took all the saddles and bridles off and turned them out one at a time, to make sure that each in turn was safe. Dolly thought that all her Christmases had come at once.

"I would put her in there too," said Mr Nix, "But she doesn't want chasing about at her age."

"Where do you keep him?" Mrs Nix asked Petra when they were all settled round the kitchen table. She told them that he was stabled at Solcum Farm. They listened to her story as she recalled how she lived in North London, but had moved the horse to the Midlands near to where her Grandmother lived. She had another horse, and would bring him up here when she finally moved. Full livery was expensive she confessed, but now that the nights were drawing out and the weather improving, she would start looking for somewhere suitable. He could be out on grass, she told them.

"He must have a good sense of direction if you have only been here for a couple of weeks," Lucy suggested.

"He is an intelligent horse," replied Petra fondly.

"She told them that Bobby was her 'forever horse,' her 'once-in-a-life-time' horse. "I couldn't part with him," she said, "not ever."

"We are full up at our yard or you could come to us," Sarah said.

"Oh, I'll find somewhere, but it is a challenge coming back and forth. I'm not up here very often, obviously. That's why I have had to keep him at full livery." Mr Nix wanted to know if the pigs had anything to do with this. "Pigs?" Petra wasn't sure what had frightened him. "It might have been pigs, I just heard a rustling in the bushes, and he spun round on me and took off. It took me completely by surprise, as he is not usually like that."

"There are pigs loose hereabouts," explained Hayley. "We saw them not long ago, and they scared Tambourine to bits; she just took off too, but I didn't fall."

"You did a dirty hang-on." Sarah piped up cheekily.

Mr and Mrs Nix recalled the morning when they woke up to see the pigs digging up their beautiful lawn. Mrs Nix collapsed laughing as she told them how Mr Nix had gone out in his pyjamas to chase them away. One of them had shot under the horse drawn scuffle hoe and, being too big to fit in the gap, had carried the hoe several feet before breaking free. "Three of the tines had dug into the lawn, a bit of the lawn that was previously undamaged by the pigs. The tines made great furrows in the turf as the pig dragged it a few feet," she explained.

"It's not a bit funny," said Mr Nix.

"Believe me, it was," chuckled Mrs Nix. "Anyway, we have a fence round the tended part of the garden now, and we had to have the whole lawn re-laid. It cost a fortune. That bit wasn't funny."

* * *

The girls rode back with Petra and Bobby, to keep them company and make sure they arrived safely. They told her all about the area and some of the history attached to Kinver Edge. As they rode past the nuclear bunker in Drakelow, Lucy told her this was a fantastic maze of World War Two tunnels, having been excavated in the Forties as a shadow factory for Rover, who built aircraft engines for the war effort. In later life, during the Cold War, it became a command centre. Unknown to them at the time, the tunnels were currently enveloped in a shroud of secrecy, as plans were being hatched in Whitehall for them to become an alternative seat of government under the instructions of the new Prime Minister, Mrs Thatcher.

"It looks spooky," Petra observed.

"It is spooky," said Sarah.

Back at Chestnut Farm, they all talked with enthusiasm about the day's adventure. Petra's story left much unsaid, and they still had lots of questions in their heads to ask. It seemed the more she told them the more they wanted to know. Why was she moving to the Midlands? It seemed like she had the perfect life down South in North London, or was it South Hertfordshire? She never clarified that. She rented out her own livery yard, apparently, and it gave her a good living she had told them. Why would she want to leave it all behind? There was more to Petra than meets the eye, Lucy told them. "I can tell something's not right," She said, adding: "I'm specially trained, so I am a good judge of character."

"Yeah, right," said Steve, sarcastically. "Of course, you are."

Chapter Ten

A Game of Cops and Robbers

Easter came early that year and springtime was barely waking up. There was still a chill in the air, although the spring sunshine was becoming more normal. Lucy had a great fondness for this time of year. It marked the anniversary of when she first realised that she was in love. Steve had been a 'stand-offish' kind of feller when they first met: aloof he was, and she didn't much like him at all. But that was then, and this is now, and now she liked him very much indeed. It wasn't so long ago that she had slammed the door in his face when he was right behind her, following her through it, and she pulled it shut after her so that he walked right into it. She smiled to herself at the memory. It had served him right for grassing her up to the sergeant, when she had been late to take control of a school crossing.

To mark their anniversary that Easter Sunday, Steve took Lucy out for an Indian meal in Kidderminster. The evening was to celebrate their first anniversary of being together as boyfriend and girlfriend. Lucy considered herself to be very lucky to have found such a soulmate, and Steve thought that Lucy was just the best friend he had ever had. Outside, he fired up the Harley and Lucy climbed aboard onto the pillion. "Steve?" she posed the question, "Can we go back to Kinver via Windsor Holloway?"

"Any particular reason?"

She shouted back to him through her full face helmet. "I just think it is always a good idea to take the opportunity of passing the stables, if it's not out of the way. We don't have to stop, just check the gate is still locked and all looks well."

"Good idea, my Darlin' Girl," he replied and they set off down the A449 towards Chestnut Stables. The motorbike popped noisily down the quiet lane. The single headlight picked out the grey outlines of ghostly trees that formed a tunnel of branches ahead in their pathway, leaving black nothingness behind them. As they approached the farm entrance, both of them were stunned to see the silhouette of a figure climbing over the gate. The figure turned, startled by the noise, and stared at the two pairs of eyes in helmets peering back over the canopy of their balaclavas.

As well as the figure climbing the gate, they thought that they saw a second person already in the yard, but they couldn't be sure. Steve made one of those decisions which could be argued as the wrong one. He drove on past the farm and stopped his bike, parking it in the driveway of the lock keeper's cottage. Lucy was cross. "Why the hell didn't you stop? We have to go back. Now, Steve, now!"

"Listen," he argued, "We'll go back through the field. We can loop back around the lock keeper's cottage and over the stile. If we creep up round the back we can find out what they're up to."

"Up to no good, I shouldn't wonder," Lucy mumbled.

"Take your helmet off, but keep your balaclava on, it will help with the camouflage." Steve instructed her. "We'll leave the helmets here, under this bush." He spoke in hushed tones. He was keen to catch them red-handed and make an arrest; though how he was going to hold on to them, with just the help of a slip of a girl, and get them back to Stourbridge police station with only two wheels, he had yet to work out.

Climbing the stile, Lucy was conscious of spoiling her black leather trousers. The stile was covered in wet green algae from the winter dampness under the trees and thick hedging. Furtively they continued along the inside of the hedgerow that divided the fields from the road. Ducking into the back of the hay barn they could see torchlights dodging about around the yard. They were perfectly hidden, dressed in their black motorbike leathers, and they followed the cover of the haystack, getting ever closer to the stables.

The beam of a torch flashed in their direction and they heard a voice say, "See what's in the barn, Tom." Steve grabbed Lucy's arm and pulled her between two stacks of large hay bales which had been neatly stacked by the forks of a tractor, but not so tight that there wasn't room for a couple of slim characters to hide between. The sound of rustling footsteps on the floor littered with loose hay and straw came nearer to where they were hidden. Lucy and Steve instinctively turned their faces away as the torch flashed across them in the gap.

They were barely visible and went unnoticed by the intruder who called out to his accomplice. "There's nuffin' werff havin' in 'ere, Nik, all the 'ay is them big bales." And he trudged back the way he had come. Steve and Lucy tried to get closer to listen to what they were saying, but they were speaking in muffled voices, although they thought that they could identify the traveller dialect. They heard a stable door being opened and listened carefully to what they thought were words of appreciation that the head collar had been left hanging outside the stable.

Lucy was horrified they were going to steal a horse, and she made a move to intercept them, but Steve stopped her. They spoke no words, they dare not and, in stunned silence, they heard what sounded like two sets of hooves being led to the gate, the sound of the gate being lifted off its hinges, followed by a clatter as it was thrown to the floor.

Hearing the horses being led down the lane towards the canal, Steve finally spoke. "Right, they have now committed a crime. We can cut them off, if we hurry." The two of them hurried quietly back down to where they had left the bike. As they reached the bottom, they were just in time to see the white flashes on Magpie and Cosmo's stark grey colouring, being led away along the towpath on the other side of the canal from the lock keeper's cottage. They were going towards the Horse Bridge. They reached the slimy green stile, and with considerably less consideration for her trousers, Lucy slid over it and followed on, barely keeping up with Steve. "Quick," he instructed her, "We'll cut them off, they must have their horsebox parked down the Horse Bridge Road."

They slithered down the track onto the lane as fast as leather gear would allow and, firing up the Harley, Lucy leaped aboard and they flew, in blind panic, up to the top of Windsor Holloway. "There's that motor bike again, Nik," Tom observed.

"Decent folk should be a-bed at this hour," Besnik Claydon replied, brushing aside any implications that there might be for him. They marched purposefully onward with their stolen horses.

It was just a matter of a few hundred yards along the A449 and Steve and Lucy were cautiously making progress down to the Horse Bridge, not knowing what they might find. When they pulled up outside Donna and Pete's house, there was nothing to find. No horse box, no horses, no horse thieves, nothing, no one. They were baffled. Steve hushed Lucy and strained his ears for any giveaway sounds, and thought that he could hear horses trotting but it was very faint. Their eyes met in bewilderment: Lucy's eyes spoke of fear and panic, while Steve's blazed with irritation and puzzlement. Then Magpie whinnied, a loud shriek of a whinny that split open the darkness, and it told them everything that they needed to know. They had taken the bridle path to the back of the hotel at the bottom of Dark Lane.

Lucy noticed that there was a light still on in Donna's house, and she knew, with dazzling certainty, that they could not do this on their own. "I'm going to get Donna." Lucy said purposefully and ran up the driveway without any discussion and banged on the front door. It was not so much a police officer's knock; it was more of a 'horses being stolen now' sort of a knock. Lucy was in a cold sweat, her mouth was dry, and she was frightened.

Donna answered the door in her dressing gown. "LUCY!" she exclaimed, "Whatever is the matter?"

"Can we use your phone please Donna? Two of the horses have been stolen." Lucy was gabbling, "They are getting away now. I am sure that they have gone along the path to Dark Lane' I heard one of the horses whinny. We thought that the horsebox would be parked here, but it's not. ...."

"Whoa, Sweetie!" Donna was puzzled but Steve was there beside Lucy in a moment, and quickly explained.

"We need to ring the station. We need some back-up to catch them." Donna didn't hesitate and Steve got straight through to the reserve and told them what had happened. They said that they would be straight out. There is nothing, but nothing, that a policeman likes better than the chance of feeling the collars of thieves, especially if it involves a chase. Within nanoseconds, the area car was screaming out of the police yard in Stourbridge, flashing the blue light and sounding the two tones: DA DAH, DA DAH, DA DAH, DA DAH, DA DAH, followed by the Black Mariah, with its gong accompaniment: CLANG A LANG A LANG A LANG A LANG. Making the rear were two panda cars, every nut and bolt straining to keep up with the convoy. All were heading for Dark Lane in Kinver, but they got there too late.

Steve and Lucy were there just before them but they were too late as well; there was no sign of a horse box or trailer anywhere. Steve took his helmet and balaclava off and ran his fingers through his hair. Lucy put her head in her hands and began sobbing. "Do you know who they were?" The sergeant asked them.

"We could hear Christian names, that's all," said Steve, "Tom and Nick it sounded like, whoever they are."

Lucy looked up suddenly from her sorrows, "Not Nick as in Nicholas, but Nik, as in short for Besnik. I bet you that was Besnik Claydon."

"You could be right Lucy," said Steve and he quickly recapped the essential elements of the story so far to his colleagues. "We have to get to Jenny Walker's Lane on the hurry up. It's a gypsy camp near Perton," he told them. "Perton?" the sergeant questioned, "That's off our patch. It's not even West Midlands. I'll get hold of the boys in Bridgnorth on the radio, and they can deal with this," he suggested. Steve threw his hands up in despair, telling them that they should all just go there now, and insisting that they had to leave immediately. The sergeant disagreed, and told him that there was nothing to stop him going, or Lucy, if they wanted, as they were not on duty. "That's Staffordshire Constabulary, for goodness sake, Stephen. It's not even the same police force."

"I'll tell you what I'll do though." The sergeant was not an unreasonable man. "Here's my radio. So long as you return it before the early turn officers come on duty in the morning, you can borrow it. It might help you." Even so, this was highly irregular and Steve thanked him, saying that he was a true Christian, and stuffed the radio inside his jacket. He and Lucy took off, bound for the gypsy encampment, with more to think about than he could cope with at one o'clock in the morning. Lucy had a great deal to worry her, too. She was eaten up with frantic thoughts for the safety of Cosmo and Magpie. How was she going to tell Sarah that she had actually sat and watched them go? It was all too terrible to contemplate. Sarah would never speak to her again. How could she have done this to her own sister? She sobbed into the back of Steve's shoulder as they hurtled north; she sobbed for Sarah and she sobbed for Magpie and Cosmo.

Steve pulled up at the entrance to Walker's Farm and considered his options. "I don't want you to go in there, Lucy," he told her. "It's too dangerous." Lucy didn't want to be left alone outside but she realised that Steve was right, and that she could well prove to be a liability.

"How are you going to get in there?" she asked, composing herself from the explosion of tears. "Without waking anyone, I mean, because your motorbike is so noisy?"

"I'll have to leave the bike out here. I would be happier doing that if you could stay with it." It seemed to Steve that this was his only option if they were going to find Cosmo and Magpie. He fumbled inside his jacket and pulled out the police radio that the sergeant had given him. "Here, you keep this with you. Get hold of Stourbridge and ask them if they have alerted the Staffordshire boys yet, and find out if they are coming to assist us? I thought that they would probably be here by now." He gently kissed Lucy, and made his way along the cart track that led to the encampment, staying close to the hedge where the shadows were darkest.

Lucy resigned herself to what might become a long wait, and dutifully called up Stourbridge to find out the estimated time of arrival from Staffordshire Police. "They will be coming from Cannock," he told her, "and the estimated time of arrival is about

1.30am." She couldn't believe that the nearest operational station was at Cannock. Goodness knows! Wolverhampton is only just down the road.

"What about Wombourne?" Lucy argued.

"Their only panda is off the road," the sergeant replied. Lucy looked at her watch and thought that this was twenty five minutes too long. But it was what it was, so she just had to hope that Steve would be alright. She was not only frightened for Cosmo and Magpie, but also for him now.

Steve stealthily made his way around the first caravan, parked within its own allotted area, dotted with pot plants decorating the frontage along with a life-size manikin of Elvis Presley. He was surprised to notice how neat and tidy the dwelling looked, even in the gloom of the night. The next caravan had a dog kennel outside and, as Steve drew closer, the dog woke and looked at him with interest. He held the palm of his hand up to the dog to indicate that he wished it to remain calm. Unbelievably, the dog remained calm and rested its chin back down on its paws. Steve expelled the air in his lungs out of relief, and moved onward. He could see Besnik's BMC lorry parked up outside the caravan at the end of the lane and, finally reaching it, he felt the bonnet over the engine. He had expected it to be warm from its recent journey, and he was not disappointed. The engine was still hot, and he thought that they could not have been far behind them when he and Lucy had followed. He glanced at the caravan nearest the lorry, where he could see the soft gas-fired lights that were still on behind the fancy scalloped curtains. He quietly opened the groom's door at the front and peered into the back, thinking that there was a chance that the horses were still inside. They weren't. He looked around for possible places where they might be, but could see nothing that would hide two lively horses.

Suddenly, and these things always happen suddenly, a dog barked and two or three kicked off in answer to the call, raising the alarm. "MEN!!" The dogs were shouting to their owners in unison: "THERE IS AN INTRUDER IN THE CAMP!"

Other caravan lights came on and began to flood the cluttered frontages. Then a powerful floodlight came on, lighting up the whole yard and the door of Besnik's caravan opened. Steve jumped behind the BMC and flattened himself along the side of the cab, tucking himself into the niche of the suicide door. This was certainly turning out to be suicide for him; at least, that was what he was thinking, when a gnarled voice whispered in his ear: "And what are YOU doin' 'ere, Gorjer?" he growled, addressing him by the derogatory name that travellers kept for those who weren't travellers. Steve had no convincing answer and just stared, wide eyed at Besnik, who was standing there in his string vest and breathing halitosis fumes into his face. Judging by Steve's leather motorbike jacket and trousers, he knew with all certainty that this was the rider he had seen in Windsor Holloway, not an hour ago.

Steve thought that he had better come clean, "Where are our horses?"

"What horses?" Besnik replied. By this time, most of the menfolk were out of their caravans and closing in to support their friend. A dog was on a line of rope, fiercely snarling and being allowed to come so dangerously close, that Steve could not take his eyes off him. All the men were shouting at once:

"Oo is 'e, Nik?"

"Who are yer, Gorjer?"

"You move, an' me dag bites ya"

"D'ja want 'im dealt wiv, Nik?"

They were all baying for Steve's blood like wild dogs themselves, and it took everything Steve had in him to remain composed. He pulled out his police warrant card and held it up in front of Besnik's face. "The horses that you stole from Chestnut Farm." He replied standing his ground.

"So......." they viewed Steve with renewed interest, ".......you're a copper?"

The others mocked Steve's upper class, accent, and the name of the 'chocolate box,' farm he mentioned. "CHestNUt FAaaarm?" they jeered, "very posh." And began to poke him in the arms and chest.

"You're not much good on your own though are ya? Eh, Filff?"

Besnik stabbed his index finger at Steve.

"What have you done with our horses?" Steve persisted.

"I don't know what you're talkin' about," said Besnik as Steve was pushed and poked out into the centre of the yard. He felt helpless and very vulnerable. This was a situation he was struggling to get out of, and he had left Lucy out at the entrance, all on her own.

Lucy, however, was being kept entertained by making friends with the two coloured horses that were tethered on long chains, along the verge.

Steve held up his hands in resignation, and said he was sorry he had intruded. But he was steadfast in his determination not to lose face either. "I know it is you that's got our horses. I will find them, make no mistake, and I'll get you too." Steve looked directly at Besnik. This last little threat was a step too far for Driscoll O'Brian, the Midlands champion prize fighter, handier with his bare knuckles than he was with polite conversation. He stepped forward to invade Steve's personal space, full of confidence and rippling biceps. He extended his arm out, so that his fist touched Steve's cheek gently enough. He twisted his wrist in a circular motion, back and forth, tickling the overnight stubble that was starting to grow on Steve's cheeks. He grinned the grin of the triumphant, and Steve stared back into his hollow eyes, and at the grimace that told him what was coming. Then, with the speed of a raptor dropping on its prey, Driscoll's elbow bent right backwards, his arm shot out forward, and his fist connected again with Steve's cheek; this time not so gently. Steve hit the ground with a force so violent, it knocked him out cold!

"Quick!" instructed Besnik. "Drag 'im over to my pick-up truck." And two or three of the men began to manhandle Steve unceremoniously towards the vehicle that Besnik used for general work and scrap collection.

"Watcha gonna do wiv 'im, Nik?" Dricoll asked, grabbing Steve's wrists.

"I'll tek 'im into Wolverhampton, and dump 'im there, the police 'ull think 'e's drunk." Besnik thought this was the best plan he could come up with, given the time allotted.

In the nick of time, police sirens could be heard in the distance as Steve groaned a waking grumble. The men were unperturbed at first, but the sirens got louder and this time the sound became so loud, that it gave them merely seconds warning before three Cannock police cars and a black Sherpa van came into view, rounding the corner and under the bridge. Headlights and blue lights flooded the already well-lit yard, screeching to a halt before uniformed policemen spilled out of their vehicles to take charge of Steve's dreadful situation.

"Thank God for the Cavalry," Steve murmured, before blacking out a second time.

Chapter Eleven
Out of the Shadows

Lucy paced up and down for what seemed an eternity. She had watched the police cars from Cannock go past her and into the camp at great speed. Finally, she decided that with other police officers present, it would be safe to go and see what was happening. She didn't like leaving the Harley, but she took the keys out of the ignition and sallied down the rough track. Before she got to the first caravan, she was overtaken by an ambulance, all lit up like a Christmas tree, with the blue light flashing. Lucy began to run.

Steve was being rolled onto a stretcher as she reached his side. Her first question was: "Where are the horses?"

Steve couldn't speak very well, because he was in such a daze and his head was spinning. "I don't know," he whispered.

Her next question was to ask who had done this to him. "Driscoll O'Brian," was Steve's brief answer. He knew the man because he had arrested him once before, for bare knuckle fighting. The Staffordshire officers had now arrested Driscoll for assaulting a police officer and bundled him into the police van.

"Don't worry, Colly," Besnik shouted after him. "We'll see you right."

"You!" shouted Lucy. "You are one of the horse thieves! Where have you hidden them?" Everyone, police and travellers alike ignored her plea.

"What about the horses?" Lucy was frantic.

"What horses?" one of the Staffordshire boys asked.

"Our horses, the ones they stole," Lucy was exasperated.

95

"That's the reason we are here."

"We can't be messing about with horses," another replied.

Lucy had further questions and wanted to know now what she should do with the Harley Davidson. A kindlier Bobby in blue said that he could help. It was a lucky accident that he had a motorbike licence and offered to take the bike back for safe keeping. Lucy dutifully handed over the keys, and climbed into the ambulance to go to the hospital with Steve.

* * *

Early the following morning, the sun was beginning to break over the horizon, bright and sparkling, fresh with a late overnight frost. Lucy was dead on her feet. It had been a long and stressful day, followed by a long night. She had waited with Steve while the doctors had examined him, taking his blood pressure and heart rate before settling him in a hospital bed till the morning. A police car from Stourbridge came out to collect her and take her home, and she had the opportunity of returning the police radio to her sergeant. By the time she fell through the front door, she was beginning to slur her words with tiredness. Kate greeted her at the foot of the stairs, having been unable to sleep properly until she arrived back safely. Lucy's eyes swam in front of her; she felt like a zombie. Kate, being her Mother, could see all of this. There's not much you can hide from Mothers.

She wasted no time in putting her to bed with a bowl of porridge and a cup of hot milk. Lucy barely finished both before she was asleep, and stayed so almost until lunchtime.

Blinking awake, she stared blankly at the shaft of light that had squeezed its way through the gap in the curtains. She watched, mesmerized by the dust particles floating like fireflies, alight with reflection. Lucy's brain was also on fire with reflection. She could only think of Sarah, Magpie and Cosmo, and Steve too. She thought of poor Steve, lying in a distant hospital. Radar was curled up on the bed beside her and, hearing her wake, he licked away the dried tears on her cheek in comforting communication. Lucy pulled on her dressing gown but, before she got to the top of the stairs, she could hear raised voices in the kitchen. Sarah was throwing a tantrum.

With great difficulty, Kate had broken the news to her when she had woken up, telling her what had happened that night. The conversation was not a good one. Sarah was overwhelmed by the fact that Lucy and Steve had watched the horses being led away and, seemingly, done nothing. "How could they!" she shouted at her Mother. "How could they just stand by and do nothing."

"It aye their fault, Bab. They core stop 'em teckin' them 'osses."

"I would have!" Sarah was inconsolable.

"Sarah, Sarah, I am soooo sorry." Lucy rushed to her distraught sister. "There was nothing we could do. Really there wasn't. We were dealing with violent people. Believe me. Poor Steve is in hospital as we speak."

Sarah broke down, flopping onto the kitchen table. She buried her head in her folded arms and wept. Lucy sat next to her and put her arms around her. "I've lost Cosmo too, but we'll find them. We've got to find them. We got Maisie's horses back, didn't we?" Lucy brushed aside her own tears. "I can understand you being cross, but we are a force to be reckoned with, aren't we? It'll be alright in the end, you'll see." Lucy wept openly with her sister. "I'm so sorry, Sarah." She kept saying over and over. Sarah said she was sorry too, and they hugged each other until the sobbing had stopped.

"C'mon, you two, enough of this. Do yo' know enough about this mon to arrest him fer theft yet?" Kate was a practical lady.

"We do now, Mum," said Lucy. "Good Lord, we saw him take them, but I want to find Cosmo and Magpie first, and I have a feeling that he will lead us to them."

"I can help you," Sarah was keen to do something positive. "We can go out together round the lanes and look for the horses ourselves. They can't be far away," she reasoned. Lucy agreed that was a good plan. In fact, it was the only plan.

Lucy and Sarah searched the lanes all around Pattingham, spiralling out as much as the roads would allow, towards Bridgnorth to the West, and Wolverhampton to the East. They saw coloured horses on scrappy little corner paddocks that were only fit for pigs, and they saw many gypsy cobs tethered on long chains on waste ground. They had no doubt that Besnik Claydon had something to do with all of them, but they couldn't find Magpie or Cosmo. They couldn't find them anywhere, and even though the nights were drawing out, by 6 p.m. it was too dark to see anything, and so they returned home to Kinver.

Lucy wanted to see how Steve was, and rang the hospital. They told her that he had been discharged, so she jumped into her car and went to the police section house, taking Sarah with her.

"Area search, no trace," Lucy told him, using police speak, as soon as she arrived, finding him in the canteen.

"I am really worried now," said Lucy.

"And me," Sarah grizzled.

"Give him some slack, is my advice," said Steve. "They didn't arrest him then?" Lucy explained that they didn't seem in the least bit interested in any stolen horses, as they were more concerned about arresting Driscoll. "Serves him right," Steve muttered. He was pleased to report that his headache had finally left him. Lucy felt the bump on his head where he had hit the ground, and admired his thick lips and colourful blue and red eye bruising.

"You look like a bank robber," she laughed, as if bank robbers all had thick lips and black eyes.

Steve stared back at her, one eye half closed with the swelling. "Very funny," he said.

Lucy gave him a hug and stroked his head, kissing it better. "It's not permanent," she smiled, "and you are still my handsome bloke."

"It's Wednesday the day after tomorrow," Steve began. "We should go down to Southall market. Have you got Polly's telephone number? Ring and tell her what we are planning to do. She will be an extra pair of eyes for us."

"It's funny you should say that, Steve," Lucy told him. "Because Polly was planning to take me with her this week, anyway."

"Really?"

"Yes, really. Remember we talked about this a few weeks ago?" Lucy reminded him of the time when they had been looking for Maisie's horses.

"Yes, I remember."

"We should take Sarah with us too. It is the Easter holidays after all, and she will be beside herself if I don't let her come." Lucy looked at her little sister, sure that she would want to be there. Steve was uncertain. He thought that the only way to travel was by Harley Davidson, but Lucy was adamant that he should not ride his bike until he was fully recovered.

"You go with Polly, and I'll take Sarah on the bike," he suggested, brightly.

"No way, Soldier!" Lucy was horrified. "We'll all go in my Cherry, and that's final."

* * *

That same ill-fated Easter Monday, in the early morning, Besnik Claydon had finished his breakfast and ventured out to check up on the horses from Chestnut Farm. He opened the ship container and threw a couple of sections of hay into the depths. That would keep the blagdon and her mate happy for a few hours. He had only stolen Cosmo because he knew that horses liked the company of their own kind, and the valuable blagdon pony would be easier to handle if she had a friend with her. "I'll get that grey screw gone as soon as," he thought to himself as he busied himself with buckets and stuff. He had hoped to ship Magpie off to Kent, where his cousin could keep her while she bred foals for him. Foals that were the right colour, just like her. Foals that would be high steppers, just like her. Foals he could take to Appleby Fayre and would fetch good prices. He had been confident that she would never get discovered, because the police were useless at finding stolen horses, but now he wondered if she was just too hot to handle.

Thomas Smith, Besnik's partner in crime, was leaning against the lorry, watching his mate tending to the horses. He told him that he thought he should get rid of them both, while the going was good. They had no idea that Besnik had been caught on CCTV with Maisie's horses. How could they? One thing was certain, though, Besnik was convinced that the blagdon and the grey were safe from discovery where they were, in the shipping container by his caravan, but he also knew that they couldn't stay there. He opened the door once more to top up their drinking water. He turned to Tom and said, "I'm goin' to take them both to Southall Market tomorrow. You're right, Tom, they're too 'ot to 'andle."

"They are now there's a copper involved," Tom agreed.

"'Ow was I to know that covi was a copper," said Besnik. "She's one o' them at Ross, I knowed she were. I doe forget a face."

"I'll come wiv ya, if ya like, Nik."

"Bostin'," said Besnik nodding approval as he slammed the door shut on the two ponies.

Magpie and Cosmo were bewildered in the dark. They had no way of knowing what lay ahead for them and they were frightened. The air was thick with the smell of ammonia and stale dung, and the filth balled up under their feet. They huddled together for warmth and emotional comfort. Still with their winter coats, the patchy sweating underneath had been damp and hot, but now it was damp and cold. Cosmo shivered with cold and fear. Magpie was a calmer individual and became a rock for her, nibbling Cosmo's neck along the crest and on her withers. She responded as horses do, and together they waited, in the dark and the damp. They waited for they knew not what.

* * *

The large chiming clock in the bar of The Navigation struck eight o'clock, as the Chestnut Farm crowd began to arrive for a regroup. Everyone had been amazed at what had happened. Hayley was quite stunned, and Donna resolved to have the crime prevention officer come and visit the stables to advise them on better security. It had taken three of them to replace the heavy wooden gate when they found it lying on the ground. Peter repositioned the hinge pins on the gatepost, so that they were facing different ways, and the gate could not be lifted off again.

Polly turned up unexpectedly, thanks to the phone call that she'd had from Lucy. "If Jim Bannister is on duty tomorrow, then there is a better chance of you getting them back safely, and arresting that thieving gypsy." Polly was adamant about the mounted branch officer's talents. "He has an unparalleled ability to track down a horse thief. I bet there is not a dealer that goes there regularly that he doesn't know," she told them.

"I cannot believe how disinterested Staffordshire Constabulary were last night," said Lucy.

"They don't understand horses," Steve defended.

Maisie was equally dismayed when she heard, but had encouraging words to say. "You got my horses back for me. You two are amazing and I am sure that you will find them. You will, of course you will."

Chapter Twelve
The Romany Way

It seemed forever that Lucy had been driving her car through the built-up streets of London suburbia. She had never been to the capital before and could not believe how vast it was. Houses upon houses, industrial factory sites, one after the other, and shopping malls by the acre. Steve and Sarah were expert in their knowledge of navigation, or so they thought, but a heated discussion of conflicting advice filled Lucy's ears, until finally she had to tell them both to shut up.

At long last they pulled into the yard at Southall police station and, filing through the back door, they were wondering where they were to go, when they were challenged by a young constable coming down the corridor.

"Can I help you?" he asked, and Steve got out his warrant card from inside his jacket, and showed it to the young man. "You are a long way from home," he remarked, and Steve told him why they were there and asked him who should they see. The guys from the mounted branch were still up in the canteen, he told them. "And where do you fit into all this, young lady?" He said directing his comment towards Sarah.

Lucy introduced Sarah. Sarah smiled and nodded. "She is the owner of the other horse."

"And our informant," added Steve, lying slightly to give credence to Sarah's presence so that they did not object to a twelve-year-old being in the station.

"C'mon," he said, "I'll take you up to the canteen." And they followed him to the lift which climbed to the floor above. Two mounted police officers, in plain clothes, were standing by the window that faced over the High Street to the market entrance across the road. Steve and Lucy expected to find them idly drinking tea, but no, they were usefully employed watching the proceedings in the street. They were watching the dealers as they came and went through the entrance of the market, conveniently right opposite the police station. Nathan Turner, the scruffiest boy you could wish to meet, and well-known for his criminal activity, disappeared towards the shops up the High Street. Steve broke their concentration by introducing himself.

"Hello," Jim Bannister greeted them, "I heard you were coming. Your cousin told us this morning." Jim introduced them to his colleague. "And this is Ashley Tyler." They all shook hands as they announced their respective names. "Hello, young lady," Jim smiled at Sarah. "Don't worry," he reassured her, putting his hand on her shoulder, "we'll get your pony back for you."

"We've heard much about your successes," Lucy was enthusiastic.

"That's encouraging," Jim smiled at them, "encouraging that other forces are taking notice."

"I wouldn't go that far," said Steve, and he chuckled at his own little joke.

Jim noticed Steve's black eye. "That's an impressive shiner you've got," he said. "Where did you get that from?"

"You should see the other two fellers." Lucy laughed.

"I had a bit of a run-in at a traveller camp near us. Driscoll is a prize fighter," Steve explained. "He can certainly pack a punch."

"It looks like he can," said Jim. "I didn't realise that a little sheriff's outfit, like Birmingham, could be that exciting," he added undiplomatically.

"Umm, very funny, we do have our moments," Steve was still smarting from his cousin's comments about sheep rustling.

"You make me laugh, you do, Steve," Lucy wagged her finger at him. "It's perfectly acceptable for you to send the Midlands up with your self-deprecating humour, but not for anyone else to do it, eh?" Steve pulled a face at her.

"We will be going over to the market shortly," said Ashley. "The saddlery sale starts at 11a.m."

* * *

Deep in the heart of the market, Magpie and Cosmo stood tethered, side by side, among some of the early arrivals waiting to go under the hammer later that afternoon. Besnik was giving the horses a final brush up when he was approached by another dealer. "She move well?" he barked the question.

"She do." said Besnik.

"Stepper is she?" he continued.

"She is." Besnik's clipped answer said it all.

"Can I see 'er movin?"

"Nope. You can tek ma word fer it." Besnik did not want to draw attention to his presence there. He wanted the horses to go quietly under the hammer so he could slide secretly back into anonymity. The other dealer wandered away but returned minutes later with an entourage of interested parties. They all wanted to see how she moved. They all wanted horses that were fast and furious, horses that could bend at the knees, horses that could cover the ground at the trot like no other. This was different to pacing, whereby the horse moves his legs laterally: the right front and hind and then the left front and hind. A stepping horse is a horse that trots traditionally enough, with the diagonal legs working together, but with immense speed and high kicking action like a Hackney, with the knees almost touching the chin. It was a very flashy action and the travellers liked that. They liked that very much indeed.

"There 'aint time, the biddin' 'll start soon, won't it?" Besnik protested.

"They sell the saddlery first, Mate. The hosses ain't sold till this afternoon." The spotted neckerchief-clad dealer informed him. Besnik's disappointment showed all over his weather-beaten face as he came to terms with staying in that god-forsaken hole for the best part of the day.

"What yer frightened of?" they asked, "Is she mad? You can't 'old 'er can ya!" They concluded.

"I can 'old er." Besnik was cornered.

Knowing that flashing a horse down the high street was most likely against the law, the dealers tried to reassure him. "They don't al'ays come to market, thems 'orsey rossers." They said. "Them foot fellers, don't care, too busy drinkin' tea." They continued on, "aint sin 'em yet anyways, don't reckon the're 'ere this week."

Besnik turned to Tom for back-up, but none was forthcoming. "Just tek 'er, you'll be back before they realise," said Tom. So reluctantly Besnik untied the lead rope and led her out into the street.

"She'll go well if you ride her," he suggested to Tom. "You're younger and fitter than me."

"What, with just a head collar?" Tom seemed dumbfounded.

"You do it all the time at home," Besnik pointed out to him. Tom shrugged, and leapt onto Magpie's back in a single bounce.

* * *

Back in the police canteen, the good guys were still looking out of the window. Sarah and Lucy gasped in unison as they saw Magpie appear out of the market. "That's my pony! Sarah exclaimed, "that's my Magpie!"

"I don't know the rider at all," said Jim shaking his head.

"I don't know him either," said Lucy, worried that they had got their assumptions all wrong.

"I know Magpie," Sarah piped up, "and that's definitely her, that's definitely my horse!" Just then they saw Besnik Claydon appear through the crowd; he was watching Magpie and Tom.

"That's him!" Lucy was excited. "That's him, the bloke who took our horses!"

"His name is Besnik Claydon," Steve volunteered, "and he is most definitely our horse thief."

"Is he indeed?" Jim's eyes lit up at the thought. "That's the name his lorry is registered under anyway, but he uses false names.

He was Bevan Cooper at Ross-on-Wye, several weeks ago."

"And that's my pony!" Sarah said as if no one had heard her the first time. She cupped her hands in front of her face, as if in prayer. Lucy put her arm around her and smiled sympathetically. They continued to watch through the window and, sure enough, they saw Tom and Magpie clattering back down the High Street, the crowds parting just in front of them. Magpie was in a muck sweat, and her little legs were rattling away underneath her, barely visible in the blur of speed. Her head was high and her eyes were rolling, as if in despair, flashing the whites as she looked from side to side to balance the motion of her high stepping legs. She was not used to being treated so roughly.

"Come on," said Jim, "let's go and make some arrests." And without haste, they went purposefully down the three flights of stairs, out into the street, across the road and into the market. "Spread out and see what you can see," said Jim. "Try not to get spotted but it doesn't really matter if you do, your Besnik Claydon and his side-kick are as good as nicked. Find where your horses are tethered and report back to me. They should be putting the lot numbers on the horses' rumps soon," he advised them. "We need to know what the lot numbers are as soon as, so watch and wait, ok?" And they all dispersed into the market place.

The sale of the saddlery was well under way, with harnesses and saddles, and any amount of horse brasses and single collars of all sizes: the plethora of leather gear and associated goods went on and on in an endless line. The auctioneer was working his way along the lots surrounded by a throng of enthusiastic bidders.

"We must see if we can find Polly's lorry," said Lucy, as they watched Jim, Ashley and Steve disappear into the auctioneers' office: Gibbet, Swag and Sons. The name of the company was written in large bold copperplate above the doorway.

"That's appropriate, Gibbet and Swag," remarked Steve, "for an auctioneer who harbours horse thieves."

"I don't think 'harbouring' is quite what they do," replied Jim, who held Mr Swag in high regard. He didn't wish to compromise his good relationship with the auctioneer, with such careless talk.

"Polly was right," said Sarah, as they dodged round the corner, "there's the fish and chip wagon." Several people were tucking into their half pints of jellied eels out of plastic cups. The girls saw the opportunity of getting into that corner out of full view from the market, and they tucked in behind the chuck wagon, and watched from the safety of their cover. They were overwhelmed by the market buzzing with travellers and dealers, and all busy with their private agendas. Big men and small men, grey hair and long hair, the very old and the very young, but the common denominator was clear. They were all working people, horse dealers and the like, all dressed roughly, be it a threadbare jumper and stained jeans, torn at the knees, or a collarless shirt and waistcoat and twill breeks that had seen better days. They all cut a similar dash, many carrying walking sticks or riding crops. Many of the dealers wore little neckerchiefs around their throats, a plethora of patterns, some paisley, some spotted, and some so grubby the pattern had long disappeared under the film of grime. There were sideburns and moustaches, some beards, and all had weather-beaten, lived-in faces. Lucy was beginning to question the wisdom of bringing her kid sister to this unseemly place.

Many deals looked as though they were being secured before the bidding for the horses even started. They watched spellbound as trilby hats and flat caps bargained heatedly, before spitting on the palms of their hands and slapping them together to seal the deal. They looked towards the lines of steel rails where ponies and horses were tethered under a corrugated tin roof. More horses and ponies were arriving to fill up the gaps. At the far end of the market, practically out of sight, there was a small collection of compounds, where stallions and scrubber colts could be confined safely without being tied up. As time marched on, the market filled to bursting point with horses and ponies of every description. One hundred and fifty lots that day, the maximum number for a small market like Southall. There were ponies and horses and dealers everywhere. The market was heaving.

They could see Polly's little lorry, full of saddlery, parked alongside a couple of other wagons, and you wouldn't think it possible to fit in the space. Sarah and Lucy went purposefully over to where Polly was parked, making their way through the crowd, dodging a bonny gypsy woman selling puppies and a man of diminutive stature with snakes in a shabby wicker basket. A lanky member of the auctioneers' staff came past Polly's truck with a bucket of glue and a satchel full of oval numbers. He began at the end of the line of horses, slapping a number onto each rump in the line, Magpie and Cosmo included.

Polly was so pleased to see them and wasted no time in telling them that she had seen their horses. "They are here, your horses are here," she greeted them excitedly.

"Yes," said Lucy, "we knew Magpie was anyway. Have you seen Cosmo then?"

"Yes, she's over there," and Polly pointed to where they were both tethered. Sarah was just desperate to run and hug her pony. "No!" Lucy was firm. "No, Sarah, you must not go to her, not yet." Sarah went into something of a sulk, turning the grooming brushes over in a box to distract herself from any temptation of expressing her feelings.

"They've been flashing her down the High Street. Poor Magpie, she looked a right mess when they brought here back. I don't know why they do that." Polly was familiar with the routine.

Sarah pulled a face. "They want to sell them, I suppose."

"We watched them from the window of the police station. It made a distressing sight. There is no time to delay, though, Polly," Lucy told her. "We have to get the lot numbers, but we don't want to be spotted by Besnik." She looked around furtively. "Polly, can Sarah and I hide in here please, while you go and get the lot numbers of our horses for us? We need to tell Jim and Ashley which ones they are, and give them an idea as to when they are due to go in the ring."

Polly didn't think they needed to worry too much, as the bidding was not due to start until two o'clock, but she saw no reason to delay and it took no time at all for her to establish the numbers and return to the lorry. "They are going into the ring early on, but the bidding for the horses doesn't start for another couple of hours. You don't want them going in the auction. You have to stop them before that."

Lucy agreed and, peering out down the side of the lorry, she saw Ashley talking to one of the more trustworthy dealers. "That's Romany Joe," Polly whispered to her, "he's ok." She caught Ashley's attention, and beckoned him to join her. He and the stern faced man came up the ramp together, and Polly nodded recognition to the horse dealer.

"You can speak in front of him," Ashley told them and so Polly gave him the numbers without preamble.

Just then Ashley's attention was taken by someone in the crowd. It was Nathan Turner, who they had seen through the window making his way up the High Street. "Where did he get that jacket from?" Ashley asked a rhetorical question. "He was not wearing anything so posh when we saw him earlier."

Sarah and Lucy turned to look in the direction and saw Nathan sporting a lovely new sheepskin jacket. "He's been shopping, that's all," Lucy said. They watched him with interest as he mingled through the crowded market place, strutting his stuff and looking particularly pleased with himself. Nathan joined his Dad, who was engaged in bidding for some harness. As he turned his back to Polly's wagon, they saw what looked like a large price ticket hanging down the back of the jacket, with the word 'SALE PRICE' clearly visible.

"What an idiot," Ashley laughed. "He's been shoplifting. Sorry ladies, sorry Joe, duty calls and my fingers are itching: I just have to feel his collar," and he went smartly down the ramp and over to where Nathan was standing, and whispered softly in his ear. "Where did you get that jacket, Nathan?" Without hesitating, Nathan tried to make a break for it, but Ashley was too quick for him and pinned him up against the railings, where a row of Indian leather bridles were waiting for the auctioneer's gavel. Ashley gave him a word-perfect caution, always recited when making an arrest. "Nathan Turner, I'm arresting you for theft of that jacket. You're not obliged to say anything unless you wish to do so, but anything you do say may be taken down in writing and given in evidence."

"It's a fair cop, Guv," replied Nathan, or at least, that's what Ashley wrote down as his reply, and he whisked him away to the charge room at the police station across the road.

Chapter Thirteen

Down Market

Steve, Sarah and Lucy were the only ones who knew what Besnik Claydon looked like. They congregated in Polly's lorry and discussed their options. "He's nowhere to be seen," Steve was dismayed. They had asked Romany Joe if he knew him, but Romany had confessed that he did not know the name, and he did not know the face either when he had seen Magpie being led out of the market to flash along the High Street,.

Jim asked where Ashley had got to, and they told him that he had made an arrest and taken his prisoner back to the station.

"Who has he arrested?" Jim was surprised, and Romany informed him that it was Nathan Turner. "That little tealeaf!" he exclaimed. "Good for Ashley."

"It was really funny, actually," Steve laughed. "He had nicked this sheepskin coat from a shop along the Broadway, and was wearing it, still with a large sale ticket with the price on, dangling down his back." They all laughed at Nathan's crass stupidity. "He might as well as been wearing a sandwich board saying, "Arrest me! I'm a thief."

"Huh!" laughed Polly. "The Irish tinkers are known for their Irish stew."

"Irish stew?" They all looked at her bewildered.

"Irish stew in the name of the law." Polly grinned, and they all groaned.

"Ashley will be back in plenty of time," Jim assured them. "Everyone will be leaving the market shortly anyway. They will be selling the vehicles in the street." Lucy and Steve were surprised. They had no idea that this was a transport market as well. Jim laughed. "You name it, they sell it," he said. "If you go right over to the back of the market, you might find a few pigs and chickens." A line of open-mouthed faces, like a row of buckets, looked back at him.

A loud, hand-held brass bell rang out a mellow donging sound to herald the start of the next auction, and most of the dealers followed the auctioneer onto the street, Romany Joe included. Some dealers had remained, mingling around the horse lines. They watched from the back of Polly's lorry as some deals were made before the auction; with the slapping of each others' palms between buyers and sellers, and much verbal animation beforehand. The seller making outrageous claims about the ability of the pony, and the buyer insisting that he would take the screw off his hands for a fair price. "The pony is a sound as a pound," they heard one of the dealers say.

"And that's all I'll give ya fer it," replied the interested party.

"Put a babby on its back and it'll do dressidge fer yer." The dealer, undaunted, continues to expand on the virtues of the pony he was trying to sell.

"Look at the damn screw," the buyer replies. "Never sin an 'oss more bandy as this 'un." The pony is then sold, despite the difference of opinion, and is led from the mart without fear of being checked out or any paperwork signed. Everything came and went from the market, seemingly without intervention from the auctioneers, although Mr Swag had eyes in the back of his head and not much got past him and his staff. All the dealers knew this.

Some horses arrived, six or seven at a time, being led by one person. Some were unloaded in the sale yard, clearly unhandled and fighting like wild things. Steve thought that this all looked really haphazard, and how they ever kept up with the comings and goings, he could only be left to wonder.

Lucy thought that it was strange that they could not see Besnik Claydon anywhere, and said as much to Sarah, who was becoming rather overwhelmed by it all. Steve was concerned that they would not be bringing this man to justice after all. "Unless, they have seen us first, and they have cut and run, knowing that they would be banged to rights. " With sudden inspiration he added, "I'll tell you what, I'll take a run down the service road where all the horse boxes and trailers are parked up. I'll see if I can see his truck."

Lucy urged him to be quick. "We will need you here, Steve; with Ashley gone, now there's just us."

Steve didn't have to go far along the service road in The Broadway, where he saw Claydon's BMC parked ahead, with its distinctive threepenny bit cab and suicide doors. He could see two men in it, eating what looked like a packed lunch. He quickly ducked for the cover of the other lorries before he was seen, and concluded they would, indeed, be back for the auction.

Steve returned, and gave the girls glad tidings, "They are still here. They are hiding in the lorry, and I could see them having a spot of lunch."

Jim suggested that they too should grab a bite to eat, and they could do that in the market, while it was quieter, instead of going to the police canteen. "The fish and chips are good here," he recommended. "Or jellied eels?" he posed the question to Sarah, and she responded by pulling a face that any gurning professional would be proud of.

"I would like to try some," Lucy bravely suggested, and Jim nodded his approval. They bought what they wanted to eat, getting fish and chips for Polly, before going to join her in her lorry.

"There are a couple of interviews I must conduct before the day is out," Jim told them over lunch. "You could be a help to me, Lucy, if you want to." Lucy held aloft her thumb, affirming her agreement, as her teeth did battle to separate out the bones of the eel that was rolling around inside her mouth. She extracted the delicate section of offending vertebrae and threw it into the nearby rubbish bin, from the top of the ramp. "Bull's eye!" said Lucy, and she did the same thing with the skin that she had peeled away with equal skill.

"Some folk eat the skin," said Jim.

"Do you?" Lucy asked.

"No, I don't like jellied eels at all." He laughed at his own cheek, having persuaded Lucy to have a taste of something he didn't like himself. "But each to their own."

"It's a shame that your lorry is full of saddlery, Polly," mused Sarah. "I don't know how we are going to get our horses home."

"There is bound to be someone going north," Jim suggested. "We can check the auctioneer's register to see if there is anyone listed." Then, in a flash of inspiration, he said that Romany Joe would know. "Romany knows everything, I'll ask him when they all return."

Jim and Lucy left the group to continue Jim's enquiries, leaving Sarah and Steve to further absorb the ambience of the market. Lucy asked what purpose Jim wanted her to serve, not that she was objecting to a bit of sleuthing. She loved all of that. "I have some questions to ask this one bloke, if I can find him. They will be awkward questions and, if you are by my side, you will be a good distraction. You don't have to do or say anything, just stand there and look lovely. While I am trying to extract honest answers from him, he will be distracted by you. It will put him off his guard, and I can catch him on the hop, so to speak." Lucy tagged along very happily, feeling like a real detective. "They don't refer to you as the 'Peeler Dealer' for nothing do they?" Lucy teased.

"Is that what they call me?" Jim was amused.

"Indeed they do," said Lucy.

Steve was downing the dregs of his tea, when they saw a fully uniformed policeman coming into the market. It was Steve's cousin, George, proceeding, as they say, towards them. They greeted each other warmly, calling each other 'Cuz!'

Polly thought that it was very interesting to watch the difference in attitude from the remaining dealers to a police uniform in the market. There was no doubt that the mood had changed. They became guarded and furtive, with sideways glances towards George, who appeared totally unaware of all this. He appeared not to notice. He was probably used to it, Polly thought.

Sarah tugged hard on Polly's jumper, barely able to speak with the impact of what she could see. Magpie and Cosmo had been untied and were getting into line ready for when bidding would begin. At that very moment, Mr Swag emerged from the office, ringing the big brass hand bell to alert the buyers that bidding was about to commence.

DING A DONG - DING A DONG - Ding a dong – ding, leading the entourage that had followed him out. They began to gather round the narrow rat run of a passage that passed for a sale ring. The horses were led, at the trot usually, up and down with the auctioneer calling for bids. The first horse was trotted towards the auctioneer's rostrum by the young man who did all the running up for them. He was a demon with the horses and fit as fit to keep going at that pace all afternoon. He showed his skill in handling just about anything; the willing and the wild. Some believed he could even make a lame horse run up sound. They were all trotted up to the auctioneer's rostrum, and back down again, twice. Sometimes, a small and scruffy lad ran behind, beating the horse on the rump as it ran, if he thought it should be going faster, or moving better. Several of the gathered throng leaned over the railing and flapped their handkerchiefs at the horses or waved their sticks in encouragement. There was a great deal of shouting, other than the bidding, "Oi, oi, oi, oi, oi," they shouted, and all for no good reason that Lucy could see. How Mr Swag could hear the bids over the din was a mystery. Perhaps he didn't! He just looked for waved hands in a certain way, or a look from a dealer with a certain expression. Then he took the bid he thought was appropriate. Maybe he pulled bids out of the air to run the price higher, maybe he didn't. But at some auctions they did that, and you had to be a canny dealer to get wise to these tricks.

Lucy and Sarah continued to watch from the safety of Polly's horse box. "Besnik must have slipped back into the market unseen," she said, but now Lucy could see his sidekick, Tom, standing ready with Cosmo. He joined the back of the queue of waiting horses and ponies as Lucy looked anxiously at the boys, willing them to intervene. She turned to Polly and Sarah, and whispered, "Be ready, they might need our help!" Sarah couldn't take her eyes off Magpie.

Tom waited patiently in line for Cosmo's turn to enter the rat run. He suddenly spotted the uniform and became extremely agitated. He looked ready to abandon the grey and make a run for it but just then, the girls saw Romany go over to him, and engage him in conversation. "My goodness!" Lucy exclaimed, "that dealer is going to warn him."

"He can't be," said Polly, "I know him, and he's ok."

"Look!" Lucy was sure of what she saw. "What else can he be saying to him?"

But Romany was not warning Tom at all. He had spotted his agitation and seen fit to intervene and persuade him to stay in line before he made a break for it. "What's to do, Mate?" he asked. "Oh, the uniform?" he continued in mock realisation. "Don't worry about him, they come in here from time to time to 'ave a look round, till they get bored, an' leave."

Tom visibly relaxed, but it didn't last, as the two cousins appeared at his shoulders, taking hold of his arms as a physical restraint to indicate the arrest. Steve began to give his address. "I'm arresting you for aiding and abetting the theft of..........," began Steve, but Tom shook free from the restraining hold and made a break for it. Steve and George failed to hold him and Tom made good use of the crowded passage to gain ground. Cosmo was left abandoned until Romany grabbed her lead rope to hold her safe. As Tom tried to flee, the crowds parted for him and, on seeing the uniforms, closed behind him to block the passage of the two policemen.

"He's a wrong'un, yelled Romany. "Stop 'im. He ain't one of us. Stop 'im, STOP 'IM!" His voice, deep and husky though it was, rose to fever pitch, and this helped to check the crowd who were keen to prevent duty being done. But there were now yards between them and Tom's escape looked positive.

As they reached the entrance of the market, there were no people to hinder the arrest, or to impede Tom's getaway either. Tom's path to freedom looked certain until Ashley, having finished dealing with his arrest, crossed the road and rounded the corner just in time to stop him in his tracks. Tom tried to jink to one side, but Ashley jinked too and they continued this dancing ritual for some seconds before Steve came tanking round the corner. Just as they reached the street, Steve launched himself into mid-air in a true rugby tackle, and landed grabbing Tom by the ankles and bringing him to the ground. A right royal punch up continued until George piled in to help. Tom took a swing with his fists and connected with Steve's face: the side of his face that was not already black and blue from the previous punch up.

* * *

"Grief, I hope they catch him," thought Lucy, as she watched them disappear out of sight. Sarah, however, was still watching Magpie, and was aghast to see Besnik emerging from the crowded horse lines with her, making his way purposefully towards the exit of the market.

She grabbed Lucy's arm. "LOOK!" she shouted. "He's taking Magpie away!"

Lucy and Polly, now alerted to the new danger, shouted above the din of the crowd to Jim, just coming out of the auctioneer's office. He was hampered by his lower position, and could not see what the girls were shouting about. His passage through the crowd was not so easy either. It was a very full market again and everyone knew who they were: plain clothes or not, it did not hide their identity.

"Romany!" yelled Polly, and Romany Joe turned, but he did not understand what she was trying say and couldn't hear her either, as the noise was so great. In any case, he was stuck holding Cosmo, and began to make his way to take her to Polly's lorry for safe keeping. All bidding had ground to a halt as no other horses stepped up to be sold. Mr Swag waited patiently for the hubbub to settle down, suspecting, correctly, that the policemen had caused the break in proceedings, and were now busy doing their job.

The three girls ran down the ramp and gave chase, just keeping sight of the flash of white hair at the top of Magpie's tail, as she was disappearing towards the High Street. Jim saw them just too late to be effective. The girls were pushing through the crowds after

Magpie, watching her back end begin to bounce with the motion of her trot. "We've lost her," said Lucy.

"Over my dead body!" shouted Sarah, and she lengthened her stride and caught up with her pony. "Whoa, Whoooaaa, and waaalk.....woooorrrrrk." She tried to instruct Magpie to stop trotting onward, holding fast to her tail, not at all confident that this would work. But Magpie had come to trust Sarah as their relationship had blossomed, and she did slow to a walk. Possibly she was fearful of another session of flashing and she ground to a halt. In fact, she planted her four feet firmly in one place, and refused to move another step.

Besnik pulled harder on the lead rope, getting cross with this stubborn horse. "C'mon, ya dam' mule," he shouted and, raising the short cane he was carrying, he turned to face her and began to give her what he thought she deserved. Sarah was on him like a wildcat, grabbing hold of him, she kicked him in the shins. He fought back, so she dug her nails into his arms and, using her weight, she tried to get him off balance, but she was too slight and he was made of sterner stuff. He flayed at her with his cane and she clawed at his face, scratching at him, and pulling his hair. He punched her in the belly, and she doubled up without letting go of him. He wrestled her to the ground and as she fell, she was able to pull him off balance and he fell on top of her with a thump so hard that, for a moment, she was winded. He raised himself above her and began striking her hard across the face with the flat of his hand. Sarah caught hold of that hand and she bit it; she bit it very hard indeed, and he yelped with pain like a puppy.

Magpie stood bewildered, until an unkempt little traveller kid took hold of the lead rope and held her safely. Lucy flung herself onto the writhing man, 'kicking and a-gouging in the mud and the blood and the beer,' she thought to herself. Pushing him over onto his side and off Sarah, she got hold of his shoulders and pinned them to the ground. Sarah had swivelled round and was now on top of him with her legs astride his body, sat across his torso like she was riding a horse, Besnik's legs kicked about wildly to no avail, until Jim caught up with them and, in his usual gentlemanly fashion, crouched down and held his ankles together firmly. Lucy leant forward and muttered those words that all policeman just love to say: "You're nicked." she said.

Chapter Fourteen

A Case to Answer

Cosmo and Magpie were together again, in one of the small compounds inside the market, and safe from further harm. There was a substantial chain and padlock securing the gate. Besnik and Tom sat side by side in the charge room while the charge sergeant prepared the papers for charging them both with the theft of two horses. The theft of Maisie's horses would come later, and be taken into consideration when they appeared at the magistrates' court. They knew that the game was up and sat silently, resigned to their fate.

Steve and Lucy signed as arresting officers, which meant that they would have to give evidence the following day. "We'll come on the train," Steve suggested. "It'll be much easier." And Lucy pointed out that if they did that, they could claim the ticket price back from the police force. "Job done then," said Steve, clearly in a jocular mood. The sergeant on the phone asked if there was anything else he wanted to add to this, and Steve chuckled that he and Lucy would have to be at court with the prisoners the following day. "So Lucy and I will not be at work tomorrow." Their sergeant sighed in resignation, and asked again if that was it. "Nope," Steve was beside himself with glee, "I'll be putting in a claim form for the train ticket, Sarge." If they could have seen their sergeant on the other end of the phone, they would have witnessed him holding his head in his hands, and shaking it slowly in mock despair. "It's been just the best of days," Steve said, grinning at Lucy as he put the phone down.

* * *

Not wanting to call Donna to come and fetch them if they could help it, they returned to the market to see if they could solve the transport problem. Sarah climbed over the gate into the compound and she could not stop hugging Magpie. She was so happy that it was only a matter of time before both of the horses were safely back home. Once she had satisfied herself that Magpie was at long last safe, she began to look around at the rest of the horses waiting to go under the hammer. There were not so many left now and there was more space to move around. Sarah felt sorry for some of them, looking neglected and unloved. Some were really nice-looking animals. There were a several palominos, and there were many coloured horses, blue and white, chestnut and white, all things dappled and brindle. Sarah's artistic flair rose high in her and she whipped out a little Instamatic camera she had and took some pictures, wishing she had brought her sketch book.

She went to the front of some of them to fuss their ears and make friends. Running her hand down the crest of a rather nice palomino pony, her hand ran across the horse's withers and she felt something sticky. She stopped in her tracks and looked at the palm of her left hand. It had traces of light tan boot polish smeared across her fingers. She looked about her and saw Steve coming to find her. She called to him in dismay. "Steve!" she exclaimed. "Come and look at this." Steve knew straight away what this meant. It didn't take much rubbing with some tissue, to reveal the freeze mark underneath. This pony must be stolen too.

Steve shook his head in disbelief. "It seems nothing is safe round here?"

"There speaks a man with two black eyes," Sarah chuckled.

"Tut, very funny. Come on, let's go and see who has brought this horse."

Armed with the lot number and the freeze mark, they made their way back purposefully toward the office, meeting Jim and Ashley on the way. They explained what they had seen. "Happy days," said Jim. "This has turned out to be a very productive day." Ashley volunteered to go over to the police station and ring the freeze mark register to check the pony's number.

A scruffy kid in his teens nearly bumped into them as they rounded the corner on their way to the office. Their eyes met for a fraction of time, and Jim muttered a half-hearted acknowledgement of recognition. "Nat?" he nodded. "You all right?"

"Alright Mr Bannister?" Nat nodded back, before he evaporated into the tethering area.

Jim watched him go. "I am going to keep an eye on him," he told the others. Jim watched Nat disappear into the horse lines, now almost empty of horses. He emerged again shortly with the pretty palomino pony, sporting a newly revealed number on his withers. This was certainly enough for Jim to act on his suspicions, "Who brought that pony here, Nat?" The lad denied understanding the question, saying that it belonged to no one until it had been sold. Jim asked him who was he working for, doubting that the boy had brought the pony here himself. "Did your Dad bring you, Nat?" Nat looked at his feet and mumbled a weak denial. Then, with no prior warning, he suddenly dropped the lead rope and took off, quickly followed by Jim who caught him by the arm. "Not so fast, Young Man."

Meanwhile the pony wandered aimlessly. "Oh my goodness," said Polly when she saw it, and skipped down the ramp to catch it and secure the rope to the side of her lorry. Steve and Sarah joined Polly and the palomino, not wanting to jinx Jim's investigations. "What an interesting day this is turning out to be," Polly observed.

Nat's father intervened, "What's going on, Mr Bannister?" And Jim wasted no time in explaining the facts. Robert Williams flatly refused to believe that the pony was stolen, "I bought 'im in good faiff," he insisted. Jim had learned over the years that it was not always the best plan to be in such a hurry to make an arrest. He was fiercely aware that they policed the market, both with the consent of the auctioneers and the dealers who frequented it. It seemed to him that the best place to get at the truth was here and now, in the market. He invited Robert to come with him to the now deserted, chuck wagon, and bought them each a cup of coffee. Lucy rounded the corner and Jim gestured to her to join them. He gave her that look that said he just wanted her to stand there and look pretty.

She was busting to tell Jim that they had found transport for their horses. Romany Joe knew this guy who had come from Telford, and had gone to find him. Jim continued with his questions; "Tell me what you know then, Robert. What's the crack?"

"I bought that pony off a girl who had a yard near me; a nice person, I thought. She said that she had fallen on hard times, had to give the yard up and was selling all her animals."

"Did you pay much for it?"

"A hundred quid," Robert told him.

"That's not very much for a pony of that quality, is it?"

"She said she was desperate. I paid enough anyways. I believed her then, Mr Bannister, and I believe 'er now. She's kosher, I'm sure of it."

Just then, Ashley returned from across the road to confirm that the pony had indeed been reported stolen to the register of the freeze mark company, but the report was a long time ago, two years or more. This put doubt in Jim's mind. He watched Robert's reaction to this news with interest, but he seemed genuinely dismayed and bewildered.

"I think it's time you came clean with us, Robert," Jim eye-balled him. "Did you have anything to do with covering that freeze mark with boot polish?"

Roberts shuffled his feet around, looked away, and wouldn't meet Jim's piercing gaze. "I didn't know the 'orse was stolen, Guvnor, I really didn't, but I did cover that mark. I didn't want any unnecessary questions. I know how vigilant you are here at Souffall. That pony would've stuck out like a sore fumb if I 'adn't. I just didn't want no trouble, and it seemed the simplest thing to do. Don't arrest me, Mr Bannister. I've done nuffin' wrong," he pleaded.

Jim assured him that he was not going to arrest him. "I know where you live, don't I?" Robert nodded his agreement. He was disappointed not to have sold the pony as he planned. He was disappointed not to be able to return with the pony either, but now that the police suspected that it was stolen property, they could not allow him do to that.

"What are you going to do with the pony, Mr Bannister?" Robert asked. Jim didn't actually know right at that moment, so he winked a knowing wink at Robert and tapped the side of his nose with his index finger. His own nose that is, not Robert's! Robert left unhappily, back to Hertfordshire.

"Cheers, Lucy!" Jim patted her on the back saying that he thought that they got more out of him than they would otherwise have done. "Make no mistake," he waggled his index figure in the air, "we will get to the bottom of this."

Lucy looked up and saw Joe coming into the market in the company of a tall man, who was smiling widely at the thought that he was going to get paid for his journey home. "Arh," Lucy said, making her apologies, "that looks like our transporter." And she left to join everyone by Polly's lorry and hear the details of the good news.

Joe introduced the man, lanky as you like, with an Adam's apple that made him look as though he had swallowed a golf ball. They all shook hands and the conversation revealed that he was returning north with an empty lorry so there was plenty of room for Magpie and Cosmo.

"I am pleased to be at your service, ladies," and he bowed before them. "Are your ponies good to load?"

"Yes, they are," Lucy and Sarah chorused. And they considered that they could load up in the road, rather than bring the lorry into the market.

The lanky Adam's apple said that he was planning to leave in about half an hour. "I will meet you back here at about 4 o'clock then." He confirmed before he beetled off to collect his money for the horses he had sold.

Polly aired her concerns. "It would be a good idea for one of you to travel with him, because you don't want them stolen again, do you?"

"It will have to be Steve," Lucy said. "I have to drive my car."

"I can go," Sarah piped up.

"Oh no you can't, Madam." Lucy was quite shocked at Sarah's boldness.

"I can follow you," Polly nodded, "but Steve should go with the horses, really he should. It would also be a help to direct him straight to your yard anyway," she argued.

"It looks like it's me then." Steve agreed. "It does seem like the only solution. I will go with him and you two can follow in the car."

"And I'll follow you," Polly grinned.

"What will happen to the little palomino?" Sarah asked, and Jim told her that Romany Joe had agreed to impound the pony at his place in Elstree until they could get to the bottom of the mystery. He said that he would have to make further investigations and follow the leads of information that he had. In the event of the pony not being the hot property that they believed it to be, Romany Joe lived not far from where Robert lived, and the pony could easily be returned to him.

"If I can be of any help, just let me know." Lucy was sorry that she did not live nearer London. This sleuthing suited her very well.

"Thank you, Lucy," Jim said, "I don't know what I could ask you to do all the way up there near Birmingham, but I will certainly let you all know what happens."

Jim was delighted that everything had turned out ok. "A good job done all round," he told them. They parted with the exchanging of fond gestures, and Sarah and Lucy went to retrieve their horses and lead them out into The Broadway. Having had previous experience of dealers' lorries, Sarah and Lucy were pleasantly surprised to see that this time it all looked in good order. There were four stalls inside so that the horses could travel in separate compartments, and this would be so much safer than Besnik's lorry where they all rattled around loose. There were hay nets still full to keep them occupied and they loaded perfectly well. Adam's apple proved to be chatty and charming, so the journey north seemed to be over in a blink before his lorry turned off the A449 into Windsor Holloway. The pretty little snowdrops in the lane had subsided back into the undergrowth, as the explosion of yellow daffodils took their place. The trees were beginning to sprout tiny leaf buds which cast a jigsaw pattern of dappled light across the road when the bright spring sunshine was at its best.

There was a welcoming committee waiting for them to arrive home at Chestnut Farm. They were all so excited to see the horses returned safe and sound. Moony neighed from the pony paddock and Cosmo answered her, which set off a conversation of neighing from the other horses, with nickering and quivering noses, all to greet the returning refugees. The children were in high spirits, fussing Magpie and Cosmo, who seemed so delighted to be back home where they belonged.

Donna wasted no time in putting the kettle on and unwrapping a celebratory cake to mark the occasion. There were lots of stories to tell as they shared the adventure, taking the micky out of Steve with his bruised face, and hearing all about the colourful characters in the market. The jaws of the children dropped open as they retold the race to stop Magpie leaving the market by pulling her tail and shouting "Whoa."

"Did she stop?" they asked.

"She did," Sarah explained, "she planted her feet in one place and wouldn't budge." Hayley was quick to point out that all that training had been a godsend, especially making her wait at the entrance to the yard before turning out into the lane. "I didn't expect the benefits to manifest themselves in quite that way," Hayley laughed. They all laughed - it was just so good to have Magpie and Cosmo back at home.

* * *

Meanwhile, Romany Joe was reversing his lorry into the gateway of his field in Barnet Lane and, having dropped the ramp, he let the little palomino into the field, where she would be safe until the lawful owner could be found. It was a pretty pony, one he would consider buying if the price was right.

Chapter Fifteen
Market Forces

The legitimate owner was not hard to find thanks to the freeze mark register but, frustratingly, all Jim's attempts to get an answer to the phone calls were in vain. Maybe the household was empty during the working day because every member was usefully employed or, he pondered further, they could be away on holiday. It was a bit early in the year, but "Hey" he thought to himself, he would just have to keep trying. His policing duties called him away from the phone to the daily 'Changing of the Guard' at Buckingham Palace, and he went to get his horse ready to leave the stables at Great Scotland Yard by 10.30a.m. He and three of the other mounted police officers would be escorting the retiring regiment from St. James's Palace down to Buckingham Palace. Riding his majestic grey police horse down The Mall, he cleared the roadway of enthusiastic tourists who milled about in the path of the bagpipe band behind him. It was loud and musically moving, and a mood of pensive reflection stirred within the souls of everyone witnessing the pageantry.

Shortly after they disappeared through the gates of Buckingham Palace, the new guard came out from Wellington Barracks with a contrasting brass band of the Grenadier Guards, thumping a rousing oom-pah-pah tune. The mood of the crowd was lifted into a jocular countenance, with striding feet that kept time with the melody, and the shoulders of those standing at the railings bounced in merry unison.

Jim took himself and his horse off to the far right-hand gate where he had a chance to reflect on the previous day. He was thoroughly satisfied with the work they had done at Southall, and he was encouraged to find two officers from the Midlands who were every bit as keen as him to crack down on this sort of criminal activity.

* * *

That same morning, those two police officers in question had taken the early train to London in time for the ten o'clock magistrate sessions at Acton. Lucy was currently referring to her notebook as she stood proudly in the witness box, spelling out in chronological order the evidence of the case. The lady magistrate listened intently to her address, while making her own notes as the story unfolded. Steve and Lucy were justified in feeling very satisfied with themselves, as they heard the magistrate's conclusion that this case was to be referred to the Crown Court, where tougher sentences could be imposed.

After Jim had performed his duties outside Buckingham Palace, he tucked his police horse up for the day and drove out to Elstree. Nicholl Farm was known to be something of a dealer's yard, and the girl who ran it seemed honest enough. Petra was levelling the muck heap when Jim's car rolled into the yard. Jim felt relaxed in her company and, drinking tea in the rest room, he listened to what she had to say. Petra remembered the pony, and said that she had bought it legitimately from Barnet Fair the previous autumn. What Robert Williams had told him was true, she confirmed: she had lost the lease to the farm yard, and she had to find new premises. She had a couple of horses she would not sell for any price, but this little pony was not one of them. So she had let it go for a knock down price. It was just as he had said.

"Didn't you think it was odd that there was a freeze mark on the pony?" Jim asked.

"These freeze marks are a load of nonsense," she argued. "You are mad to have it done, it just seals the horse's fate of getting slaughtered. They become too hot to handle." Jim pointed out that she had just handled one, and asked her who she had bought it from. She didn't know. "Just a bloke in a field, a field in Barnet where the annual horse fair is held," she said, and continued after a pause, "I'd know him if I saw him again."

Jim shook his head in disbelief. "Very useful," he mumbled sarcastically.

"I should arrest you on suspicion of theft, you know," Jim told her, and he wagged his finger mockingly at her.

Petra just shrugged. "Do it then," she laughed. "You'll end up with egg on your face, I am no more a thief than you are Humpty Dumpty."

"Why should I believe you?" Jim quizzed. "You bought a pony from a bloke who you didn't know, and had not even thought of checking out the identity to see if the pony was legitimate." He went on to explain to her how it would have been the easiest thing in the world just to make a phone call, and he admitted that he could not make out why she could not see what was staring her in the face. Even though she was a likeable girl and there was something undeniably genuine about her, he left her to consider her options, promising to be back in due course when all his enquiries were complete.

The following day Jim was back at Great Scotland Yard. He went downstairs to the sergeant's office where he could make the umpteenth phone call, undisturbed, to the pony's last known owner. Finally, there was someone at home and the phone call was answered, but what the owners had to say took the wind out of Jim's sales. "Oh yes," the voice on the phone said. "I remember the pony. It was stolen once, but we managed to recover it, thankfully. We sold her in the end because my daughter grew too big for it." Jim asked why they had not cancelled the 'stolen' status on the register. He didn't know really, and he couldn't answer that one. "We didn't get around to it," the voice said. "I probably thought that my wife had done it, and she thought that I had."

Jim put the phone down and signed a big sigh. 'The one that got away,' he thought to himself. He rang Romany Joe to tell him that

129

he had better return the pony to Robert. "I've arranged to buy it," he said. "If it all turns out ok, of course" I know of a little girl who is looking for a nice pony." It pleased him that he would be able to make her the happiest little girl in the world.

A few days later Jim returned to Nicholl Farm to report the good news. The yard was empty. All the horses had gone, and Petra had gone. There was a bonfire in a paddock burning broken pallets and furniture from the tack room, including the arm chair he had been sitting on just a couple of days before.

There was a spotty faced youth poking the fire with a mucking out fork. Sullenly, he told Jim that she had scarpered on the hurry-up to goodness knows where, and he couldn't care less. The girl had been trouble from the day she arrived.

Jim remarked that he knew she had lost the lease on this place and was leaving shortly, but didn't realise that her plans were to vacate the farm quite so soon. "Lost the lease, my foot," the spotty youth mumbled. "She's just done a runner, with no warning, and her bloke is not best pleased, either. In fact, he is in a right royal rage."

"Who actually owns this farm?" he asked.

"I told you, her bloke owns it. Well, ok, his parents own it anyway."

"No, you didn't tell me that," Jim was beginning to feel frustrated. "You just told me that she had a boyfriend and that he was cross."

Spotty stopped poking the fire. "Who are you?" he asked.

"More to the point," Jim stared into the lad's face: "Who are you?"

"Who wants to know?" he replied stubbornly. Jim dutifully pulled out his warrant card from his inside pocket and showed him. "I might have known you was the filth, comin' here pokin' about."

"So, what are their names then? These parents?" Spotty became a bit more lucid, and directed Jim to the big house where they lived.

He followed up on his investigations, and they appeared to Jim to be honest folk, ready to speak of all they knew of Petra, which was not that much. They confessed that their son had been in trouble with the police recently, and they had not seen him for a week. They clearly blamed her because she had disappeared too.

Jim thought that a trip to the police station in Borehamwood might be a good idea. He could check out some of the police records and do some digging around. If Petra's boyfriend had been in trouble with the law before, then the boys at Borehamwood would know all about it. It would have been easy for him to turn his back on this unfolding drama, but his interest was kindled and he couldn't help himself, wondering what more there was to uncover.

Jim was wading through the records when the collator returned from his break. "Have you heard of a Neil Gormley?" Jim asked him.

"Him!" came the reply. "There is a warrant for his arrest. He didn't turn up at court a week last Tuesday. He's a little toerag, involved with exporting horses for the meat trade in Europe. It is probable that he is doing this illegally but, more importantly, we are prosecuting him for armed robbery. He is a wrong'un, and no mistake."

Jim nodded, assessing the information. "Do we have a picture of him?" he asked, and the collator got out the pile of recent mugshots.

"He's in here somewhere." He thumbed through the collection. "Here we are, this is Neil Gormley."

Jim studied the picture. "I know this face," he said with recognition. "I know this face from Southall market. I will be going this week. I have not had any dealings with him, but I have seen him there. Wanted on warrant, you say?" Jim stroked his chin, "I wonder if he will turn up there on Wednesday?"

"Treat him with caution," the collator warned, "he is known to be violent,"

"Well," Jim cocked his head, "We'll see. I'll keep my ear to the ground, and hopefully I will be in touch again with good news."

He rang Steve and told him what had occurred. "So, she was hiding something then." Steve observed to Lucy when he had put the phone down. They concluded that they would probably never find out what that was. "I hate unsolved mysteries," he said and sighed with resignation.

"Neil Gormley, and Petra Featherstone," mused Lucy. "Do you remember I told you about that loose horse we found on Kinver Edge last week?" Steve's eyes invited Lucy to continue. "Well, the rider's name was Petra. It's an unusual name."

"I very much doubt that there is a connection," said Steve philosophically "You can't catch them all, Lucy."

* * *

Jim and Ashley crossed the road into the market two days later. Romany Joe and Robert Williams were in conversation by the chuck wagon. "Good morning, Gents," Jim greeted them warmly and Ashley touched his cap. Robert thanked them for not arresting him over the palomino pony and said he very much appreciated that Jim had given him the benefit of the doubt before establishing all the facts. "I usually know those who 'crosses the line' and those who are honest," Jim smiled at them approvingly.

"You look like you are on a mission this morning." Not much got past Romany Joe. Jim told them they had an arrest to make. He told them that the man could be unpredictable and violent, "so it's best you don't get too close," he warned. Robert and Romany were more than intrigued, and wanted to know who this person was, bringing trouble to an honest horse market.

The auction for the horses had started and Jim and Ashley kept themselves casual, trying not to look furtive while they scanned the dealers gathered along the run-up line. The railings that kept the crowds from the lot numbers were the same railing where the harnesses had been displayed earlier. Some bits and pieces had yet to be collected and still hung there abandoned. It was difficult to see faces, as most were leaning over the railings concentrating on the horse currently under the hammer. Neil Gormley had found himself a comfortable spot leaning over an uncollected western saddle, and was bidding enthusiastically for a brown uninspiring animal that was being run up and down the line. They spotted him when he turned briefly to see if he could identify who was daring to bid against him. His opponent was none other than the prize fighter,

Driscoll O'Brian. He had avoided a prison sentence at the court hearing for punching Steve, because of diminished responsibility, or, at least, that is what his brief had argued.

Jim and Ashley weaved their way through the crowd to get nearer him without him noticing them. Neil was intent on the job in hand. He was planning to flee the country for the last time that night, and taking another load of horses across to France gave him the opportunity of making a fast buck that he could not resist. He was concentrating heavily on outbidding his opponent and was confident he would get this horse.

Jim and Ashley closed in, either side of Neil. Jim gave the nod and they grabbed an arm each at the same time.

Neil swung round like a coiled spring, eyes alert with survival, his fists were up and ready. The attempt of arrest momentarily thwarted gave Neil the opportunity to grab his riding crop stuck in the back of his boot, and he began to lash out with it. Jim and Ashley backed away from the swinging whip, whistling as it cut through the air.

The bidding at the market had stopped, the horse still unsold, and the dealers parted away from this madman waving the crop. Jim and Ashley became the main targets, closed inside the circular space that was created around them. Hanging over the back of the Western saddle was a holster with a handgun inside.

It is a fact that, in the heat of the moment, the brain works fast but not always in a rational fashion. Neil Gormley was not the brightest of fireworks on a good day and, in a quieter moment of reflection, he would think it unlikely that there would be a real gun for sale in the auction, and he would think it unlikely that it would be left loaded. But this was not one of his most rational moments and in his befuddled brain, and in the nanoseconds that he had to make decisions, he believed this to be his passport to escape arrest.

He grabbed the gun from the holster and waved it threateningly at our heroes. The vision of this weapon shocked the crowd into backing away little further. Jim was not so easily fooled, and made a lunge towards Neil intent on grabbing his wrists and overcoming his feeble defences. Neil pulled the trigger. It was point black range and, if the gun was real, then it was curtains for Jim Bannister. But the gun was a toy. An arrow shot out of the barrel of the handgun and a flag with 'BANG' written on it in red, unfolded and fluttered in the wind!

The dealers of Southall market thought this was just about the funniest thing they had ever seen and collapsed onto each others' shoulders in fits of raucous laughter. Neil was left mortified and humiliated as uncontrollable hilarity spread around the market but, before Jim or Ashley could facilitate the arrest, a fat prize fighting finger was stabbing Neil on the shoulder. He turned and, without explanation or preamble, Driscoll O'Brian packed a punch, square into the middle of Neil's face. He crashed to the ground with a thump, and Jim and Ashley breathed a big sigh of relief. Neil was trussed up like a Christmas turkey with handcuffs before you could even say 'Who shot the sheriff?'

The bidding continued as if nothing untoward had disturbed their trading, and Neil was carted off to a police cell across the road and Jim shook Driscoll by the hand. Not knowing who he was, he showed his gratitude warmly, "Thanks mate, I owe you," he said. Driscoll didn't know Jim Bannister or Ashley Tyler either, and he was super surprised to learn that his talents had helped the POLICE.

* * *

The irony was not lost on Steve and Lucy when Jim rang them to tell them what had happened. Jim described Driscoll as a really nice bloke, which had Steve rolling around holding his sides with laughter. "So, what was Neil up to in the market?" Steve asked.

"He's a bad egg and no mistake," Jim passed judgement.

Steve was relaying the conversation to Lucy as he was speaking to Jim, as the news was so extraordinary. "I would love to have seen all of that," said Lucy.

"It is a good job you weren't there," Steve pointed out. "For a start, Driscoll O'Brian would have known who we were and I doubt he would have been so ready to pitch in and help."

"What a funny thing to happen!" Lucy nodded her agreement.

* * *

It was a bright and sunny day when Polly opened her shop 'Horses Galore' the following Saturday. Maisie stepped through the door out of the gathering heatwave that was promised for the day. "Hi, Maisie," Polly greeted her. "How are things in your neck of the woods?"

"Pretty good, thanks," Maisie replied. "I have decided to advertise for liveries. Another two horses I think, and an extra pair of eyes at the yard would be a good idea." She handed Polly the card she had carefully prepared for display on the notice board. Polly was surprised that she had room, until Maisie explained that the farmer had agreed to rent her an additional field. Maisie was a good girl. She always paid her rent on time and kept the yard tidy, and that was worth a great deal to the farmer.

"So long as you get the right person," Polly was quick to see all the advantages. "They could even cover with the feeding rota for you." Maisie agreed.

They chewed the fat for a few minutes before Maisie left the shop, bumping against a young lady in the doorway as she was coming in. "I am sorry," Maisie said automatically to her, and Petra returned the apology automatically.

"Can I help you, or are you just looking around?" Polly asked. Petra explained that she was looking for somewhere to keep her two horses, and asked Polly if she knew anywhere. "My friend has only just this minute put an advert on our board," Polly told her. "You've just missed her; she was leaving as you came in." Petra looked back at the doorway just in time to see Maisie driving out. She took the details off the card. "I have just moved up here," she volunteered. "I'm staying with my Nan at the moment and the pony is at the bottom of her garden. It's not ideal. My big horse is in full livery, but there is a limit to how long I can afford that sort of luxury." Polly expanded on how nice Maisie was, and Petra left the shop full of hope and encouragement.

Chapter Sixteen

Take it Easy

The gossip at Chestnut Farm was all about the pigs running loose on Kinver Edge. But Mr Nix was determined to do more than just gossip. With a chirpy countenance, he and Mrs Nix set out in their van for Midland Shire Farmers in Kidderminster. The country store sold everything from greetings cards to dog food, from natty little tools for castrating lambs to warm and stylish quilted jackets for the fashion conscious rider. It sold rat poison and garden rakes: everything but everything was sold at this store, and Mrs Nix was in her element perusing the shelves for some nice socks to wear inside her wellingtons. Mr Nix had gone there for one reason only; he was there to buy some pig food. He and Mrs Nix had more than they could handle with these darned pigs, breaking through the fence and turning his lawn over again. He was filled with malice and 'no more Mr Nice Guy' thoughts, confident that his cunning plan would bring an end to it all.

The wild pigs could be quite shy, so Mr Nix had to gain their confidence somehow. He was surprised how quickly they found his piles of pig nuts during the first night. He was impressed how easily he managed to persuade them to enter the shed where he hoped to secure their capture. Lying in wait halfway through the night, he furtively crept out into the garden, intending to shut the door on them, but they were cunning too. Scampering into the darkness, as his footsteps on the gravel alerted them to the approaching danger, they had no intention of hanging around and they scarpered.

Mr Nix did not give up. He decided to hang around outside and go about his business while the trap was set, putting out the bait earlier and earlier. The pigs came earlier and earlier, and got used to him hanging around and not interfering with them. It took less than a fortnight and, with the help of a friend with a livestock trailer, the first consignment of pigs were on their way to Bromsgrove and the great piggery in the sky.

The word soon got around that Mr Nix had pork for sale. Michael was sorely disappointed. "I could have helped him with the pig hunt," he said with great passion.

"I think it has more to do with enticing them into an enclosure with some food, rather than actually hunting them down" Donna explained to him.

"Why has he taken them to Bromsgrove?" Sarah asked.
"He's taken them to the slaughterhouse, Sarah," Donna said as if it was obvious. Hayley cupped her hands in front of her face; she was filled with abject horror. Donna was mystified at her reaction. "What did you expect?"

"I expected him to find good homes for them," Hayley could barely keep her calm. "That's what I expected him to do."

Donna shook her head, "It was the supposedly 'good homes' that let them go free in the first place, Hayley. They bred and numbers increased, and now they are a serious problem, you should know that. It was Tambourine who bolted with you because of them."

"Couldn't we have just taken them somewhere else to live?" Hayley was clearly very unhappy about this. "Cannock Chase is a wide-open space; couldn't we have taken them there."

"What!" Lucy exploded. "No! We couldn't!"

"That would have made us no better than the irresponsible person who let them loose on Kinver Edge in the first place." Donna was getting impatient.

"In any case," Lucy compounded the argument, "I hear that there are already wild pigs running loose on Cannock Chase, and they have enough of their own, I shouldn't wonder?"

Hayley knew when she was licked, and resigned herself to accepting the ways of the world. "I'm turning veggie," she said in protest.

"Oh really," Donna laughed, "You won't be interested in the barbeque I'm planning then." If nothing else, that got the attention of everyone there, and they demanded further information with enthusiasm. Donna explained that she had been to see Mr Nix, and had put her name on one of the pigs. She said she thought that a celebration would be a good idea. "We can invite Maisie, and toast her good fortune in her horses being recovered."

"And our horses!" Sarah piped up.

"And Magpie and Cosmopolitan Lady, of course," Donna added. "Catching the thieves, and with an excellent result at court there's lots to be thankful for." They all agreed it was a happy time for them. Gill and Michael bounced with enthusiasm at the thought of a party at the farm.

"Can we invite other people?" asked Lucy, and Donna asked who she was thinking of. "I don't know if they would come, but I would love to ask Jim and Ashley. It would be good, wouldn't it?"

"Yes," replied Donna "it would be good to invite them. They were certainly a key ingredient in your success. Peter and I thought that we could spit roast a whole pig, so there will be plenty of food to go around. In fact we are more likely to need more people to eat it!

"Can we invite our friends?" asked Sarah. "You know the friends we made along the way in finding all of the horses."

"Who, for instance?" Lucy looked down at her little sister.

"What about Lewis, and the ladies who bought Jack?"

"Stella and her Mother?" said Donna. "What a good idea, I liked them very much. They cared about horses. Yes, and Lewis too, if he wants to come."

So the scene was set. Donna and Peter took delivery of three pigs in the end. They put one in their own freezer and one for the barbeque. Lucy bought half for her mother and father. It was a win-win situation,

"Not from the pigs' point of view," grumbled Hayley, even though she and Dave had the other half pig in their own freezer

* * *

The day of the hog roast arrived and everyone was helping to prepare for the party that afternoon. The two terriers, Radar and Tetley, sat supervising the hog that was gently turning on the spit over a roasting fire. Lucy and Steve were laying out a long salad bar with a pile of crusty bread, and plates and serviettes, when they heard the distinctive sound of a Harley Davidson motorcycle popping along the lane. Steve's questioning eyes met Lucy's and Lucy shrugged as they heard the bike turn off the lane onto the gravel of their yard. "It can't be!" squeaked Lucy as she recognised Lewis' silhouette, dismounting from his new bike.

"It jolly well can," Steve said gleefully as Lewis pulled off his helmet. "Lewis!" he called and they walked over to greet him. "As I live and breathe, it is so good to see you." They dutifully admired his new bike and caught up on each others' news.

Everyone was there - friends from far and wide and families too. Mr and Mrs Tempest came from the garage up the road, and Donna's Mum and Dad would not have missed this for the world, neither would Lucy and Sarah's parents.

"Hi, Cuz!" Steve called out to his cousin George and his family as they walked through the gate, having parked their car in the field opposite. Polly Purse came too, and Maisie brought Petra who, in the end, had moved both her horses to Prestwood Drive. It was a healthy gathering. Lucy was delighted to see them, and they had plenty to chat about as the afternoon party got under way. They talked about all the happenings of the previous two months, including the pretty little palomino pony they had seen at Southall. How odd, they said, that it had turned out not to be stolen, even though the register said it was. Petra listened intently, probably with more interest than the others realised, but she said nothing.

"It was a really happy conclusion, wasn't it?" Sarah looked for confirmation, "I mean, when Romany Joe found that lucky little girl to buy it from him."

"Romany is never short of good homes for nice ponies," Polly confirmed. "Probably paying him good money too."

"I don't have a problem with that," said Maisie. "You should have invited him too, you know. He did his bit and helped out with the cause a great deal!"

"We have," Lucy told her, "and I am expecting him to come with his wife and daughters. We have invited Jim and Ashley too, and they said that they would come, but I haven't seen them here yet."

Right on cue, Jim and Ashley walked into the throng of people, warmly greeted and welcomed. "I am so pleased you could make it, both of you. Did you have a good journey?" Lucy walked purposefully towards them.

"Lucy! Steve! Polly! Sarah!" Jim and Ashley greeted each by name, those that they knew, and Jim's eyes scanned around the other guests, smiling warmly at them. For a nanosecond, his eyes met Petra's but neither of them acknowledged recognition.

"You'll never guess who we saw, heading this way up the 449" Ashley grinned.

"Who?" Lucy asked, not being the only one who wanted to hear the answer.

"Romany Joe," Ashley announced. "Romany Joe in a bow top caravan. You might have to find somewhere for him to put his horse!"

"Really!" Sarah bounced into the air clapping her hands. "I like Romany Joe."

"And he likes you," said Lucy. "What fun! Can you get a stable ready for him Sarah?"

"Is he really coming here?" she turned and asked, as Sarah dashed up to the yard grabbing Gill to give her a hand.

"He said he was," Jim confirmed. "We had to stop and speak to him, didn't we?" Then, holding his index finger in the air, he whispered. "Listen, that sounds like him now!" And the gentle rhythm of his gypsy cob's footfalls echoed along Windsor Holloway.

What a spectacular sight it made to see a genuine bow top wagon roll into the yard. Joe's face beamed through his ruddy complexion at the welcoming committee gathering to greet him.

"You must be Mrs Romany," Steve greeted his wife, helping her step down from the footplate."

"Call me Queenie, Darlin', everybody does."

"My good lady wife, Queenie," Joe confirmed, to a chorus of hellos. Without further delay, he unhitched his horse and gave him to Sarah to put in the empty stable. Magpie and Cosmo stretched out their necks over the stable door to give him a good sniff and he walked past them, not without a degree of squealing into the bargain…

The waft of roast pork began to fill the air, heralding to all that the pig was getting ready to eat. "You're just in time," Steve announced, "I think the pig is ready. Come on, let's grab some grub and find ourselves some straw bales to sit on. We are hoping Jim and Ashley will tell us all exactly what happened at Southall a couple of weeks back."

"It's a story worth repeating" said Joe, "I haven't seen anything so funny."

Petra made a feeble attempt at finding somewhere else to go but she didn't know anyone there and Maisie insisted that she stay with the group. "This should be a ripping yarn," Maisie told her, "You'll love it. Don't be silly. Please stay here with us." Petra resigned herself and gathered a plate of food, along with the others and made herself comfortable on the array of straw bales that littered the top paddock. Maybe Jim Bannister had not recognised her, maybe the penny hadn't dropped. After all she would be the last person he was expecting to see.

"Come on then," said Lucy, "What's the crack?"

"Well," Jim began, "as I told you on the phone, this feller, Neil Gormley did go to Southall that week." A shiver of fear shot down Petra's spine at the mention of her ex boyfriend's name.

"I had been warned that he could be a dangerous man," Jim continued. "But we did well, me and my mate Ash here," and he gave Ashley a brotherly pat on the shoulder. He then looked directly at Petra. "You know who I am talking about, don't you, Petra?"

Petra stared back in silence, wide-eyed with the realisation that she was rumbled. She did not know where to look, as the whole group were now looking at her. After what seemed to her to be an eternity of staring, she looked at her hands, which she was rubbing nervously together on her lap, and she ventured to speak. "Yes, Mr Bannister, I know who you are talking about."

"I think that we should hear your story first, my Dear. Don't worry, you are among friends." The others were agog with curiosity.

"Just the mention of his name fills me with dread," she confessed. "But anyway, I'll start at the beginning." Everyone was hanging on her words. "Neil and I had been together for about a year before I realised what I had got into. His parents owned the yard I was renting, and I felt really privileged to be given the opportunity. It gave me a good living: teaching children, a bit of horse dealing, a bit of breaking young horses, and selling the odd bag of horse food. I thought that I had it made. Then I found out what he was up to."

"Why didn't you just chuck him?" ventured Sarah. She was shushed immediately, and told not to interrupt.

"The horses that he bought at various sales, he would bring to my yard and expect me to break or bring on those that needed more training. There were some that were screws, you know, horses you wouldn't give house room to. Some were good looking animals. He took those that didn't sell away in batches, I thought to good homes." Petra paused to gather her thoughts. "He bought far more than we could realistically sell on."

Petra continued after another pause. "But it did suck, you know? Something wasn't right. No one transports horses so regularly and in batches of six or eight at a time, supposedly to go to good homes. He would stay away overnight on each trip, saying that he was taking them to Scotland, or to Cornwall. On a couple of occasions he said he was going to Ireland. I got suspicious, and did some digging. I found out that he was taking them all to France. They were all going for slaughter."

Hayley gasped in horror. "No!" she exclaimed, "that's dreadful, Petra," and she took another bite of her pork roll.

"It's illegal." Petra continued. "Since a new ruling two years ago, they have readjusted the 'minimal value.' It means that they have to be worth under a certain value to export for meat. Some looked like good horses as far as I could see. He was fiddling the forms somehow. But I didn't wait to find out."

"Didn't you challenge him?" asked Lucy.

"I did. I shouldn't have done. He threatened me but, more to the point, he threatened my lovely boy, Bobbysox." Petra held her head in her hands and Maisie put her arm around her. "He said that if I bubbled him to the police then Bobby would be on the next lorry to France. I didn't waste any time after that. While he was away on the next trip, I moved him up here, near to my Nan. She's quite horsey and said she would keep an eye on him. She even rode him occasionally. I told Neil that I had sold him. He didn't believe me, but there was nothing he could do."

"This was not a long-term solution, though?" Lucy observed.

"No," Petra shook her head. "It wasn't. But he was a very difficult man to disentangle myself from. I tried to leave him but he hounded me; he was very controlling."

"So, you moved up here bringing the pony too." Polly concluded the story for her.

"What about the burglaries?" asked Jim holding her in his gaze. "How much did you know about that?"

"I knew he was a thief, and a no-good, but I didn't ask questions if I didn't think I would like the answer." Petra seemed genuinely perplexed. "I buried my head in the sand, I suppose. I thought that our horses going for meat was bad enough. It told me what sort of bloke he was, and I wanted nothing more to do with him."

"Did you know that there was a warrant out for his arrest?" Ashley spoke at last.

"No, I didn't. I could have guessed that there was the occasional house breaking, if I had thought about it. He had an explosive temper, but he was ok while he was getting his own way - a good friend really."

"There is lots to think about when you look at his police records. He's been in and out of prison since he left school." Jim told them solemnly.

"Oh Lordy!" Petra was shocked. They were all shocked. "Please, Mr Bannister, please don't tell him where I am." Jim and Ashley told her that her secret was safe. They smiled encouragingly at her. "There is no fear of that, Treacle," said Ashley.

"I would think that he's looking at a long stretch in the clink."

"They should throw away the key," Sarah expanded, as if that was the end of the matter.

Petra was clearly relieved, and everyone felt happy for her. They told her that she was safe in the Midlands. "As long as you pay me your rent on time," Maisie teased, and they all laughed.

"I'm so pleased that I moved up here," Petra beamed at them all, "You are good friends. Indeed, I feel very privileged."

Donna's ghetto blaster tape recorder sang out favourites from The Eagles. Carol and Michael began dancing and fooling around to the music, 'Take It Easy'. Sarah beckoned to Gill, inviting her to dance.

"Lucy?" Steve said, taking Lucy by the hand, "Shall we?" And he gestured towards the patch of pasture that passed as a dance floor. Lucy nodded and, hand in hand, they joined the girls and Michael, movin' and a' groovin'.

Kate turned to her husband, grinning widely, "Aye this a bostin' do?" she said.

Printed in Great Britain
by Amazon

45379978R00088